The man i[n my] [line] of death, didn't have to wave knives or guns around.

I could see at once. *He* was the weapon. Possibly the scariest weapon I'd ever seen.

I could feel this as clearly as if he'd shot me where I sat.

I felt as if he already had.

He was so still as he regarded me that I began to wonder if I was dreaming.

Then he spoke. "I beg your pardon?"

His tone suggested that he'd taken a very long time to answer me because he didn't quite believe that I'd spoken in the first place. That I'd dared.

"That voice doesn't make it any better," I told him, recklessly.

I thought of my mother. How she'd seen her moment and taken it. This was not necessarily the moment taking me, but I felt that rush of adrenaline all the same. And I understood something, with intense clarity.

Demure and *mindful* are tactics we employ when we need to live, want to live, to make the living more comfortable.

They had no place here.

USA TODAY bestselling, RITA® Award–nominated and critically acclaimed author **Caitlin Crews** has written more than one hundred and thirty books and counting. She has a master's and PhD in English literature, thinks everyone should read more category romance and is always available to discuss her beloved alpha heroes—just ask. She lives in the Pacific Northwest with her comic book–artist husband, is always planning her next trip and will never, ever read all the books in her to-be-read pile. Thank goodness.

Books by Caitlin Crews

Harlequin Presents

Her Venetian Secret
Forbidden Royal Vows
Greek's Christmas Heir
Her Accidental Spanish Heir
Forbidden Greek Mistress
An Heir for Christmas

The Diamond Club

Pregnant Princess Bride

Notorious Mediterranean Marriages

Greek's Enemy Bride
Carrying a Sicilian Secret

Work Wives to Billionaires' Wives

Kidnapped for His Revenge

Visit the Author Profile page
at Harlequin.com for more titles.

SICILIAN DEVIL'S PRISONER

CAITLIN CREWS

PRESENTS

If you purchased this book without a cover you should be aware that this book is stolen property. It was reported as "unsold and destroyed" to the publisher, and neither the author nor the publisher has received any payment for this "stripped book."

Recycling programs for this product may not exist in your area.

ISBN-13: 978-1-335-21344-0

Sicilian Devil's Prisoner

Copyright © 2025 by Caitlin Crews

All rights reserved. No part of this book may be used or reproduced in any manner whatsoever without written permission.

Without limiting the exclusive rights of any author, contributor or the publisher of this publication, any unauthorized use of this publication to train generative artificial intelligence (AI) technologies is expressly prohibited. Harlequin also exercises their rights under Article 4(3) of the Digital Single Market Directive 2019/790 and expressly reserves this publication from the text and data mining exception.

This is a work of fiction. Names, characters, places and incidents are either the product of the author's imagination or are used fictitiously. Any resemblance to actual persons, living or dead, businesses, companies, events or locales is entirely coincidental.

For questions and comments about the quality of this book, please contact us at CustomerService@Harlequin.com.

TM and ® are trademarks of Harlequin Enterprises ULC.

 Harlequin Enterprises ULC
22 Adelaide St. West, 41st Floor
Toronto, Ontario M5H 4E3, Canada
www.Harlequin.com

HarperCollins Publishers
Macken House, 39/40 Mayor Street Upper,
Dublin 1, D01 C9W8, Ireland
www.HarperCollins.com

Printed in Lithuania

SICILIAN DEVIL'S PRISONER

To M and R for introducing me to *365*.

Quannu u diavulu t'alliscia voli l'arma.

If the devil pays you compliments, he wants your soul.

–Sicilian saying

CHAPTER ONE

BIRDS SANG IN the thick green trees as they danced through the dense, overgrown gardens outside the magnificent old villa some thirty minutes from the center of Palermo, Sicily. But what Giovanbattista D'Amato—called Jovi by the few who dared address him directly—noticed despite their chatter were the sounds that should not have been there, soft beneath the usual noises he knew so well.

It seemed he had a guest.

When he was not the kind of man who encouraged visitors, especially of the uninvited persuasion. Something that must surely be clear by the untended sprawl of gnarled oleander and fig trees that had grown up around the gates down near the road and made the entrance to the villa seem all the more secretive and, therefore, more provocative.

The villa was perfectly preserved and stunning, as everyone always whispered in shocked tones, *despite everything*. Teenagers and tourists who thought they might poke around a place with such a riveting, tragic past were usually scared off by their own overactive imaginations long before they made it to the villa's front door.

The ghosts that haunted the villa and its quiet slide toward a graceful, genteel ruin knew only too well how to occupy a mind and sneak deep into an unguarded moment.

Jovi knew that better than anyone.

He heard the car out in the front of the villa, on the winding drive that had given way to the demands of changing seasons and the scrubby mountainside that stretched above and below, though nothing could conceal the bones of the estate, a crowning achievement of the Sicilian Baroque period. Neither time nor negligence could dim its glamour in the slightest.

Jovi had certainly tried.

He heard the slam of the car's heavy door, yet he stayed where he was. He sat perfectly still in the shade of the towering oak tree some gardener long-dead had planted here in another lifetime, as if he was contemplating nothing more than the easy mysteries of a warm, Sicilian afternoon.

But that was only the impression others might form if they saw him here, sitting so quietly.

And only those who didn't know him.

Because anyone who knew Giovanbattista D'Amato knew exactly who and what he was. Ice, straight through.

Ice where other men were flesh. Ice in place of organ and bone.

He remained still. He supposed that it was possible that somewhere, back in the dimness of the youth he did not allow himself to recall too closely—or too often, lest he give those ghosts free rein—he had gone ahead and taught himself these skills he used without thought, now.

The ability to sit so still that the birds themselves mistook him for a statue. A stone like any other.

The capacity to wait. To do nothing else. To simply *wait*, without moving. Without breathing too much, lest it make his chest move and differentiate him from the stone walls. To easily parse the various sounds that reached his ears. The birds. The breeze and the trees above. The rustle of small creatures in his gardens, long since surrendered to riots of rogue blossoms and weeds—a rebellion against the meticulously maintained, award-winning planting concepts that had once been synonymous with the villa and its residents.

He identified all of those, set them aside, and listened for the heavy fall of a man's leather shoe inside the graceful, empty rooms of the once-proud villa that rose up behind him.

Jovi did not lock the place. Why should he? Terrible things had already happened here and there was no pretending otherwise. There was nothing to steal that he could not replace, assuming that he could be bothered. To his way of thinking, anyone was welcome to drop in. Unannounced and heavily armed, if they wished.

Though they might wish otherwise. Quickly.

He was not concerned about people entering this place where he lived when he was in Sicily. Because he knew that the difficulty was not in the entering. But in the leaving.

Once someone invaded his space, they would leave it again only if *he* wished it.

His were the only wishes that he would allow to prevail on this sprawling parcel of land, set up on the rugged mountainside, claimed by men who must have imagined it was ever truly possible to escape the chokehold of Sicily.

Jovi knew better.

He heard feet on one side of the duel staircases in their Sicilian Baroque style, all high drama as they marched away from each other and then angled back to meet at the great door.

And as the footsteps drew closer, he heard the faintest sound. Like a rough laugh, checked before it was anything more than a breath.

No need, then, to worry about his response.

He waited instead. And when the footsteps drew even closer, barely making scraping sounds across overgrown flagstones crafted by the finest stonemakers in Sicily and left to the whims of the sun, there was another laugh. This one untethered, likely because its owner thought he was alerting Jovi to his presence.

The way he always did.

"I don't know how you live in this haunted place," came the intruder's familiar, disparaging voice.

Not an intruder, Jovi corrected himself. Not exactly.

He did not bother to turn around. He knew who his uninvited guest was. Had known, in truth, the moment he'd heard that particular heavy cadence of footfalls from inside the villa.

Carlo D'Amato, his cousin. His oldest cousin and his

uncle's favorite son. This meant Carlo was also considered the *sotto capo* of what some news organizations liked to call the *D'Amato crime family*, but only because they dared be disrespectful from the distance afforded them through newsprint.

To those who knew better than to show disrespect, they were known as Il Serpente, wily enough to outwit the many criminal investigations that had plagued families like theirs since back in the 1800s. Not to mention the rival criminal organizations who muscled in where they could.

Most shivered at the very thought of Il Serpente, a true family organization built on blood ties, because blood brokered loyalty. Blood was less likely to be bought.

Jovi was a part of this family, but not the way Carlo was. Because Jovi's father, the traitor Donatello, had betrayed his own brother—bringing dishonor to the family name and very nearly handing them all over to the authorities who stalked them.

This was a stain upon them all. Jovi alone of his father's family had been spared.

So he was *family*, yes. Blood where it counted. More importantly, he was a weapon.

The weapon, perhaps.

"Did you hear me?" Carlo's voice rose in pitch as he swung himself around the chair so he could look down at Jovi from the front. Allowing Jovi to watch, fascinated as always, as this big, powerful man who feared nothing and no one—a fact Carlo liked to broadcast whenever possible—looked more than a little *wary* at the sight of his supposedly lower-ranked cousin.

The way everyone did if they had the misfortune of seeing him.

Because there was rarely any reason to see Jovi that did not involve pain.

Carlo, as ever, could not hold Jovi's gaze. He looked away, and his shoulders hunched, more signs that he was intimidated by the cousin he liked to brag that *he* did not find frightening in the least.

He even spat on the ground, as if Jovi was a superstition in need of clearing. "You're a spooky *stronzo*," he muttered.

Jovi only waited. Carlo knew exactly why Jovi lived here. This was the home Jovi's father had inherited from his own father, as he had been the oldest D'Amato son in his generation. Donatello had been too soft for the family business, however, according to the stories everyone liked to tell. Jovi's grandfather had used to say that he had two heirs.

Donatello for the public family legacy, charming and academic and sophisticated. And the crafty, cunning, and wholly soulless Antonio for the family business, where sophistication was not required but brutality was celebrated.

Antonio had wanted nothing to do with this place after he had meted out bitter family justice upon Donatello, his wife, and his two young girls.

Jovi did not allow himself to think of them in other terms. His father and mother. His sisters.

They had all lost the right to those connections when Donatello betrayed their family.

He rarely permitted himself to think of them at all.

It was his cousin who seemed to enjoy bringing up ancient history whenever he came here, always pointing out the empty, echoing rooms. Always making certain to remind Jovi of the things he opted not to remember. Or, perhaps, reminding Jovi of his roots in the only way he could without risking Jovi's displeasure.

Despite what Carlo liked to tell the rest of Sicily, and likely himself, both Jovi and Carlo knew very well that Carlo would never dare to *actually* insult his cousin. Here, in these private moments, Carlo's cowardice was always clear.

Carlo swallowed. Then took his time looking Jovi's way again. "Patri has a job for you," he said.

This, too, was obvious. Only a directive from Antonio himself could compel Carlo to visit this place of shame and despair, a stain upon the family name. There was no possibility that Carlo would ever come here to spend time with Jovi, to catch up or whatever it was people did when they had all of those social connections Jovi had never been permitted.

Even if Carlo wasn't terrified of Jovi, they would never connect in this way. Jovi shared blood with his family and their ancestors, here in Sicily and across the water in Calabria.

He did not share anything else.

That would require that he be made of something more than ice, and his uncle had made certain that he remained too cold to melt. Ever.

In truth, he preferred it that way.

Sometimes Jovi walked through the crowded squares of Palermo or drove past the beaches in summer. They were always teeming with people having their coffees and their harder drinks. Talking loudly, waving their hands in the air. Clustered together over tiny tables in public spaces or flung about in abandon on the sand, entirely unaware of their surroundings or what sort of monsters might be waiting there, watching.

Looking for a chance to strike.

He could not understand it.

Yet Jovi knew his cousin not only understood these things, but enjoyed them. Carlo maintained his never-ending stream of mistresses despite the carefully selected bride from a Calabrian family he'd married so ostentatiously in the cathedral in Palermo. Despite the vows Jovi had heard him make with his own duplicitous mouth. And the babies his dutiful wife, raised by men just like the one she married, had already provided him—three sons and counting.

Jovi did not make vows. He kept promises.

And he was not given to acts of sadism the way his cousin was.

He was Antonio's favorite form of detached and dispassionate justice, meted out in the face of betrayal, a broken word, or a disrespect too great to be ignored.

Or sometimes simply because Don Antonio felt like serving it to his enemies, with impunity.

Jovi was the final solution to problems that torturers and deviants like his cousin failed to solve.

Carlo knew as well as Jovi did that even Don Antonio took care to aim his best weapon carefully. What mattered was that Jovi was loyal. The son of a known traitor had to demonstrate his honor and devotion, without fail, forever. Even more so than the rest of the family. When he was young, Jovi had done what was asked of him—whatever was asked of him—because he'd had no choice if he wanted to live.

These days, everyone was aware that Don Antonio's orders to Jovi were a lot more polite than they had been. Or than they were to anyone else.

That was the trouble with crafting a perfect weapon. There was always the worry that it could be aimed back at oneself.

Most of the time, Jovi simply waited, letting the ice in him grow thicker by the day, feeling nothing at all.

This was not to say that he was a saint or a monk. He fucked. A lot.

There was no shortage of women who were drawn to him as surely as reckless moths to an indifferent flame. He took what he was given, left them in pieces, and never took the time to learn their names or commit their faces to memory.

Sometimes, in the middle of the night, he would dream of the boy he barely remembered, a creature of heat and need, flesh and yearning. He dreamed of a bright, wild, intense boy who had delighted his father and made his mother laugh as she pretended to look to the heavens for the intercession of the saints.

But thinking of these things in the light of day was like telling himself fairy tales, anodyne little ditties about obedience, and Jovi could not relate to them. They were not the memories he allowed himself.

Because there was nothing in him that burned. He breathed destruction and delivered pain.

There was not one part of him that was not cold.

Even Carlo, who claimed he feared no man and was the scourge of many, was always wary in Jovi's presence.

Perhaps more than simply *wary*, Jovi thought.

Clearly disliking the quiet, Carlo outlined the situation that his father had sent him to share. It was no different from every other task Jovi had been set over the years. The particulars changed, but the outcome was always more or less the same. There were many men who played these games, who waged these wars in the dark shadows where fallen men created their empires, ripped down others, and were kings in all but name. There were many men who preened in their own power, little realizing that power, like any other commodity, could be bought and sold.

Because there was always more power. There was always someone more desperate to claim it. A circle without end.

These same men never understood that they as good as signed their own death warrants the moment they started throwing their weight around, because there were always higher bidders with deeper pockets. There were always new markets with more motivated sellers.

It was only a matter of time until they were all worth more dead than alive.

"We want him to hurt," Carlo said of the man in

question today, some or other arms dealer in Eastern Europe. It didn't matter who he was, only that he'd decided he was more powerful than Il Serpente and could dictate his terms. "Eventually, he'll pay the price for his disrespect but first, a little pain."

Carlo carried himself as if he was a man of supreme beauty, though it was difficult to tell if his mistresses cared at all about his supposed good looks when his wallet was so well-upholstered and infinitely deep. He was not afraid to fight with his own hands—and, indeed, preferred it—a rarity at his level in an organization like theirs.

See again: sadist.

Accordingly, he kept himself in shape as if he anticipated that fight occurring at any time, despite his exalted position as his father's right-hand man.

It had been a long time since Jovi had heard his cousin complain to the rest of their cousins that it was difficult to keep up with his fitness when he was Sicilian, and there were too many delicacies forever on offer. Many a man had fallen into softness thanks to the preferred cuisine around the family tables and the local cafés, called bars.

The most dangerous men in the world are fat and round, Carlo had told Jovi once, his eyes dark with shame, when Jovi had effortlessly outperformed him in the gym.

Then they are not as dangerous as they think, Jovi had replied with his typical equanimity. *The men who fear them are the dangerous ones. The ones who do their bidding and could therefore do someone else's, too.*

Sometimes, like now, he thought his cousin remembered that conversation. There was something about the way Carlo refused to look at him sometimes that assured him it was something Carlo kept close. No doubt dreaming of the day that he would rule this family and give Jovi orders. Or better yet, get rid of Jovi altogether.

Jovi did not bother to inform his cousin that his loyalty was not transferable. He did not need to remind his cousin that his skills far outstripped Carlo's sick little games.

A day of reckoning would come, that was certain. These lessons could wait until then.

"Boris Ardelean is a collection of former Russian nationalities," Carlo told him in that sullen way of his, never quite able to look Jovi in the eye. "A mutt. A Czech national who should shut the fuck up, learn his place, and sell his guns. Instead…"

He shrugged. There were some who would see a shrug like that and lose control of their bowels. A shrug like that, from a man like him, had death written all over it.

Jovi was unaffected.

Carlo continued. "Instead, he thinks he can play games. He thinks he can dictate terms. He thinks he can go around the family to make his own name for himself. But… *Lu rispettu è misuratu, cu lu porta l'avi purtato.*"

"Respect is measured." Jovi agreed with the proverb his cousin was quoting. It was how they all lived. Or in Carlo's case, pretended he lived. "Whoever respects others will be respected in turn."

His cousin nodded. "Don Antonio likes his own name." The meaning was clear. This arms dealer needed a lesson. "Killing him would be too easy. How would he learn? How would he fully understand the depth of his disrespect?"

These were not questions that required an answer.

He stayed where he was, sitting still in his chair and watching as Carlo paced a little, as unable to stand still as he'd been when they'd both been small boys. Five and six and allowed to run wild while all the old women in black smiled at them and called them angels.

Only the fallen kind of angels, Jovi thought now. Fallen deep and hard, lost somewhere far beneath the surface of any lake of fire.

If he was an angel, it was the angel of death.

"This Boris has a daughter," Carlo was telling him. "He's been putting out feelers, seeing if he can marry her off in the old style to create an alliance. My father thinks Boris's only alliance should be with us."

Jovi inclined his head. "I understand."

For a moment, Carlo still stood there, staring down at Jovi, with that same wary look on his face that he often wore in his cousin's presence. To cover his uneasiness and fear, Jovi was certain.

"Other men might ask if she's pretty," Carlo pointed out. "If they might have a little fun, a little pleasure with their work. But not you."

"I do not believe in pleasure," Jovi replied. He didn't even bother to shrug. "In my work or anywhere else. It has no purpose."

Sex, killing—it was all the same to him. Women

or men, it made no difference. Sometimes there was set dressing, the better to send a message. Sometimes mementos were required, whether before or after the death depended entirely on the reasons for the death.

He felt nothing about any of these things. He did his job.

Ice was ice wherever it was cold enough.

He could see that Carlo was holding back a sneer. That his cousin dearly wished he could speak frankly to him, though Carlo would never dare. Jovi even knew what he would say, as he'd said as much to others who had foolishly relayed it, imagining Jovi was the sort of man who would make alliances.

He's a freak, Carlo liked to tell the rest of the family. *Him and his freak father. If it was up to me, I never would have let him live.*

"I'm not the one who fears death, cousin," Jovi told him now. "I don't have to dress it up and make it a game."

If he was anyone else, he thought Carlo would have lunged at him. He could see the loathing in his cousin's gaze. But then, of course, Carlo did nothing.

Because, at heart, he was a coward.

He showed this to Jovi every time they came face-to-face. Every single time.

And well did Carlo know it. Because he said nothing further. He only swallowed back whatever he wanted to say—no doubt thinking better of it and hating himself for it—and then turned around again to storm back into the house.

Jovi heard a crash from inside and assumed that

Carlo was expressing his displeasure the way he often did, because he ran hot. And if asked, could claim any damage was an accident.

Jovi, obviously, had never asked.

Carlo was a coward, but he was also dangerous. He was sick in the way many men in their profession were sick. Pain was a game to them, not a means to an end—and because of this, they would be their own undoing.

It was written all over them.

It was what made Carlo who he was. His life was a preview of how he would die.

Jovi supposed his was, too. Ice unto ice, frozen into nothing.

This was as inevitable as the death of the daughter of a fool named Boris who thought he could play games with the likes of Antonio D'Amato.

Theirs was a world with very strict rules. They were always the same rules. Death stalked them all, and none of them could escape it. None of them would.

Especially not if it came for them in the form of Jovi, Il Serpente's coldest flame.

He sat still for a while longer, until the sounds of his cousin faded away. Until the roar of Carlo's engine was swallowed up once more by the sunshine and the breeze. The careless birds wheeling overhead.

Only then did he rise and head into the villa filled with ghosts and the shattered remains of whatever glasses Carlo had thrown against the wall, so that Jovi could begin planning the most expedient way to do the thing he did best.

Because unlike his traitor of a father, when Jovi

had promised his body, soul, and eternal loyalty to his uncle right here in this villa on the night of the great brotherly reckoning when Jovi had been eight years old—he'd meant it.

CHAPTER TWO

I KNEW DEATH when I saw it.

When I saw *him*.

I knew it the way any living creature sees its own mortality come at it, implacably, in the final moment. That narrowing within. That impossible calm. *Zero at the bone*, as the poet once said.

A caught breath, a deep chill.

But it was not completely unexpected.

I figured out who my father was a long time ago. Not the specifics, not at first. Yet what was obvious, always, was that he was an unpleasant person. A bully. The sort of man who thought nothing of using his fists. The kind of man who had never acknowledged the role he almost certainly had played in the death of his first wife, my mother—if the whispers were to be believed. And in my world, they were usually scripture.

It was not a tremendous surprise to find out that he was a criminal.

He had always been one as far as I was concerned.

Even before he summoned me home from that strict convent school near Bratislava, Slovakia, dragged me before him in his study in his ugly, brutalist house outside Prague, and looked me over in a way that made my skin crawl.

It's time you stop draining the family coffers, he had told me.

I don't know what that means, I'd replied, careful not to show him too much spirit. Since this was a man who took anything but abject deference as outright defiance.

I mean that you're pretty enough. You take after your mother in that way, and God knows I've paid enough to get you more cultured than she ever was. He'd sneered. *A common bit of trash off the streets of Transylvania.*

I knew better than to react to that, the way he likely wanted me to.

What I knew about my mother was little more than scraps and whispered stories and the one photograph I'd managed to find of her. I didn't know if she was trash or not. I wouldn't have cared if she was. I wished I could remember her, but I'd still been a baby when she'd died. Disappeared. Whatever you wanted to call it.

Boris loved nothing more than to bait anyone around him, because when they reacted to him, he could call it an attack. Then anything he did was just fine. Justified, even. And I had been eighteen then, only a month away from my graduation. The last thing I wanted was to spend that last bit of time away from him under a doctor's care, recovering from a beating.

Yes, sir, I said instead, like the good little convent-trained girl he'd paid for.

And I think, looking back, that was why he let me go back to school at all. And allowed me to actually graduate, which was the only accomplishment a daughter of a man in his world was permitted. Everything after that would be the duties I was expected to perform, at his command and then, when he chose a husband for me, that husband's.

Sometimes I liked to dream that my mother had disappeared by her own hand, driving that car over the side of that embankment and careening straight on into the Vltava River herself. Whether she was thrown into the river and drowned—the official story—or simply made it look that way—my preferred narrative—she was free.

I liked to dream about that a lot.

My father had paraded me around at the slick, revolting parties he attended after graduation, often leaving me in the tender care of my latest stepmother while he talked business with men who usually looked even scarier than him. This stepmother was the youngest one yet. She was only a couple of years older than me, but I thought she might be the one who lasted. Because as far as I could see, Katarzyna had nothing in her but spite and vitriol.

That was the very least a woman would need to survive my father.

Just because I knew better than to show it didn't mean I hadn't nursed mine for years.

You are lucky, she'd told me at one of those parties, not long before my twenty-first birthday. *He is taking his time with you. He wants to make certain you fetch a good price. There are not many fathers who would do this for their daughters.*

I was under the impression he was doing it for himself, I'd replied, because I didn't have to watch my mouth around *her.*

She'd scoffed. *Men are disgusting,* she'd said offhandedly, and it made me think a variety of unpleasant things about my father—more unpleasant than usual, that was. *But it is true that if they pay a lot, they will see you as expensive. A luxury item.* She shook her head, her pale eyes on mine. *You silly girl, don't you understand? It's not a question of escaping your fate. You have no fate your father does not control. My own father sold my virginity to the highest bidder, and believe me, those bids were high.*

I'm sorry, I'd said quietly, unable to pull up the usual veneer.

Katarzyna had blinked, as if she'd never had a response like that before.

Life is too short for sorry, she'd replied, after a moment. *I had to develop certain skills. Different skills. You will not need to do that, because he is selling* you *as a bride.*

I must not have looked enthused, because she'd sighed. *Yet somehow, I know that you will not be grateful.*

She was right. I wasn't.

And I knew better than to be histrionic where anyone could hear me, but some nights over the last year—as my father narrowed down his choices and I could feel the noose tightening around my neck—I would put my head in my pillow, scream, and wish that he would just kill me instead.

I was used to death as a companion, because whatever happened, it was coming for me.

That was a fact.

Whether at the hands of one of the terrible men who watched me as they negotiated with my father for *alliances*, their eyes hooded and their mouths grim, or if I made a bid to escape the way I liked to think my mother had. Or the way a daughter of one of my father's business associates had. I wouldn't say she was a friend—our lives were too fraught with peril for that—but she had fallen in love with one of her guards and had made it all the way to France before they'd found her. Them.

I didn't like to think about that one too much.

All of this to say that when death came for me at last, I wasn't surprised.

What I did not expect was for him to be so beautiful.

"*Sakra*," I breathed out when I looked up from my book that night.

Because something infinitesimal had changed in my heavily guarded bedroom. Some inkling perhaps, if it was even that, because I heard nothing. I sensed nothing, but something made me glance up, and there he was. Standing there against the wall opposite my bed, his dark, glittering gaze seemed to wrap itself around me. Tight. *Too tight*.

I tried to take a breath and failed. "This is unfair."

I set the book down. Maybe I dropped it. There was some part of me that thought that he was an apparition. That I'd dreamed him up or he'd merely leaped, fully formed, from the pages of one of the books I liked to read—but I knew better.

Immediately.

The hairs on the back of my neck were prickling. I had sudden goose bumps, everywhere. And I didn't recognize him as one of my father's guards—the only people I saw who weren't family these days—so I knew he wasn't one of them.

Besides, there was nothing about this man that wasn't terrifying.

Including that sharp, impossible beauty of his.

It was a kind of...disheveled glory. His hair was thick and dark. His eyes were a lighter shade of brown, unreadable, and gleaming with something like a cool flame that I could feel lick all over me. His nose was a grand Roman affair and it brought his face the kind of sculpted authority it needed, because it would otherwise be too pretty. That sensual, stern mouth of his. Those cheekbones that defied gravity.

I shivered, and that was not even getting into the *shape* of him. Perfectly formed, like something out of an art book, carved by masterful hands into the sort of lyrical marble that belonged in museums.

Or shrines.

It was only after I accepted that he was, without question, the most spectacular man I'd ever laid eyes on that I noticed that there was no weapon in his hand.

Not that this made him seem any less dangerous, but it was surprising.

This was not the first time that someone had attempted to get to my father through me. I didn't really like to think about the man who'd jumped on the hood of our car one day with me and an earlier stepmother in the back. When I did remember it, what played through my head was all her screaming in Hungarian and me staring straight ahead as the man pounded his fists and that vicious-looking knife in his hand against the windshield.

If he'd been serious, my father had told us disdainfully, later, *he would have come prepared to shoot.*

I had been seven.

The man in my bedroom, this angel of death, didn't have to wave knives or guns around. I could see at once. *He* was the weapon. Possibly the scariest weapon I'd ever seen.

I could feel this as clearly as if he'd shot me where I sat.

I felt as if he already had.

He was so still as he regarded me that I began to wonder if I was dreaming.

Then he spoke. "I beg your pardon?"

His tone suggested that he'd taken a very long time to answer me because he didn't quite believe that I'd spoken in the first place. That I'd dared.

"That voice doesn't make it any better," I told him, recklessly.

I thought of my mother. How she'd seen her moment and taken it. This was not necessarily the moment taking me, but I felt that rush of adrenaline all the same. And I understood something, with intense clarity.

Demure and *mindful* are tactics we employ when

we need to live, want to live, to make the living more comfortable.

They had no place here.

His gaze moved over me like a caress, at odds with his preternatural stillness. "What does my voice have to do with anything, *baggiana*?"

What indeed? I thought. It was... Velvety. Cold, like the rest of him, but it seemed to bathe me in fire.

Especially when he called me that name. I didn't have to know what it meant. I was pretty sure I didn't *want* to know what it meant. It still seemed to burn through me like the alcohol I'd drunk only once, in secret. It lit me up and rolled through me, setting brushfires.

Everywhere.

He studied me like I was an experiment. Or he was conducting one.

"Ruxandra Emilia Ardelean," he said, pronouncing my name like it was a secret password. An incantation.

"Yes," I agreed, though agreement felt a little too much like complicity. Even surrender. "Though my friends, if I was allowed any, would call me Rux."

His dark gaze seemed to light on fire.

I followed suit.

I felt the *roar* of it wash over me, through me, then seem to gnaw its own place deep inside me.

"Then that is what I will call you, *baggiana*," he said, his voice rougher, then. Lower. Velvet after dark.

As if he was my friend in any capacity. But somehow, I didn't have the nerve to be quite so reckless as to say *that* out loud.

He was still leaning against the far wall and his very nonchalance seemed to set off a dark, dangerous rush of sensation within me. All he did was study me and I felt myself shaking, from the inside out.

As if the trembling was starting deep inside me, down low in my belly, rising like a swell of a song the longer we shared the same air. The same ferocious silence.

I didn't dare look away from him to check the clock on my nightstand but I could tell that it was late. Very late. My father had insisted that I accompany him and my stepmother to another party, and the two of them had gotten into one of their *moods* on the way back. In other married couples, it might be considered a fight. But Katarzyna didn't fight with my father. No matter how insulting he was, or cruel, she responded to him in the same deadpan, literal way.

As if he was really asking her questions. As if he was really in some confusion when he asked her things like what kind of *this* or *that*—and it was always something insulting—she thought she was.

All the other stepmothers had screamed or cried or come apart. If I could remember my own mother, I imagine she would have done the same, much as I'd like to think otherwise.

Katarzyna was, in many ways, my hero.

I tried to channel her now. I tried to arrange my features into that mask of placidity she always wore. As if it could not possibly matter what this stranger in my bedroom said or did. That he was worth as much notice as a spider that made its way onto my ceiling one night. Nothing I wanted to see of an evening, and something I would like very much to remove from my vicinity, but without any need for theatrics.

I don't know what he saw when he looked at me, but something shifted. I saw it, but couldn't make sense of it. "You must know, of course, what happens now."

I was certain I did.

"Do I get to know your name?" I asked instead of dwelling on what was coming.

Maybe that was a kind of weapon, too.

That odd, gleaming light in his gaze that made me think of liquid gold, gleaming there in all that darkness. "Why should my name matter?"

"It's only sporting to know the name of one's executioner," I pointed out with great bravado. "Surely we can agree that it's a matter of honor."

Something changed again, then. I could *feel* it before I saw anything to suggest it. A moment later, barely a breath, he tilted his head to one side.

"Do you think that will save you?" he asked, his voice quiet and mild, and far more dangerous for it. "It is only a name, after all."

"It's only polite," I replied.

That tilt of his head seemed to intensify. So did his gaze. "You can call me Jovi," he said, in that accent of his that spoke of warmer climates, olive trees, warm sunshine—

That was what the gleam in his gaze reminded me of, I realized. It was that kind of gold. It was the endless summer of a perfect, Italian afternoon. The kind

I'd only seen in movies, because I'd never been farther south than Bratislava.

He lifted a hand, and I tensed. And it wasn't that I'd *forgotten* the situation I was in, or my peril, but the reality of it all came flooding back then.

Hard.

I was expecting to see something ugly and violent in his hand—but it was only his hand.

My heartbeat didn't seem to note the difference.

"Come," he told me, and it was an order. "We will leave this place."

I did a quick calculation in my head. My father and Katarzyna would either be fast asleep or otherwise occupied. If history was any guide, my father always preferred to get his own back in their bed if he couldn't get a rise out of Katarzyna otherwise.

A daughter didn't like to think about these things, but it was unavoidable. It wasn't as if the man had any shame.

Jovi—and it should have introduced me to more shame than I already felt, the lilt I felt inside when I thought his name—could not have come in through my windows. They were facing me. Even if I somehow hadn't seen him come in, the windows themselves would have made noise. At the very least I would have seen him move across the room to face me the way he was now.

He had to have come from outside this room, having found a way into this fortress of a house that my father always bragged was impregnable.

And if Jovi had come in somewhere else in the

house, that likely meant that he would want to retrace those steps. But I wasn't sure how he planned to do it when there were so many guards in the house. To say nothing of my father himself. Just because he didn't *like* to do his own dirty work didn't mean he *wouldn't*. And he had been known, even on nights of excess, to find his way back to his study.

To count and stroke his money, I had always supposed. As far as I knew, it was his only joy in life.

"You can try to escape me," Jovi told me, as if he was there inside my mind. As if he'd found his way in, no matter how hard I tried to convince myself that, like Katarzyna, I was unreadable. Unknowable. "But as in all things, *baggiana*, there are consequences."

"Meaning you'll kill everyone in the house? You'll burn it into the ground? You'll torture me later? I'm afraid you'll have to be more specific." When his eyes seemed to widen, very slightly, I lifted a shoulder, then dropped it again. "My father is a very unpleasant man. I imagine you know that, since you're here. I'm conversant in consequences. I'm just wondering if yours are different."

"You hold the lives of everyone in this ugly house in your hands. Is that a departure for you?"

"It *is* an ugly house," I breathed, my heart still too loud in my chest. "You have no idea how long I've been waiting for someone to say it. I think the Emperor has no clothes, but in this case, the Emperor is the house, and the clothes—"

"Shut up, Rux."

He said that so calmly. That was actually what made

me go quiet. The simplicity of it. The quiet command and the fact he said my name.

Weak men shouted and lashed out. Weak men always showed their hands—usually in the form of fists.

It was crystal clear to me that Jovi was not a weak man.

"You are different, so I will explain this to you," he said.

"I'm not like other girls?" I asked brightly. "I don't know if that's a compliment or an insult."

"Most women who find me in their vicinity in this way faint," he told me in that same low voice. So mild. So devastating. *So delicious.* "Sometimes from pleasure, it is true. Sometimes from terror. I'll be honest with you, I expected you to do the latter."

"I would love to faint," I told him, and if I was a little breathless from the *sometimes from pleasure* part, well. I could lie to myself about that. "It sounds like a lovely escape from the pressures of daily life, don't you think?"

His voice was like the night, his gaze darker still. "I do not."

"Out of curiosity, how many women have you abducted?" I tried to sound nothing but politely curious, the way I might at a dinner party. "It's not that I'm checking your references or taking a hard look at your résumé, but you know how it is. Many have tried, none have succeeded, so what sets you apart?"

I thought he shook his head, slightly. When he continued speaking, it was as if I had never said a word at all. "We will exit this house. We will not make any noise. I cannot trust you to remain quiet, even if you promise to do so, as that is the nature of your situation. You may therefore choose a gag, or I will knock you out."

And when he lifted a dark brow at me, I decided that my genetics were making themselves known after all.

Because the things he was saying to me should have made me feel sick. I should have been horrified. I should have flinched away from him as he prowled closer to the bed.

I should have screamed the house down all around me the first moment I saw him.

I felt that treacherous heat move all over me, wrapping me up and burrowing its way deep inside. Deep between my legs, I felt a heat unlike any other, a kind of ripe weight, and a slickness.

And I might have been more upset about this, but I was too busy seeing myself for who I really was at the worst possible moment. All this time I had convinced myself that I was nothing like my father. That I had nothing in common with him. That I was a pure, clean, *normal* person where it counted.

But the truth was here. Right here in my bedroom, stalking toward me. Then towering over me, a column of finely wrought sculpture made man with those flashing dark eyes of his, that impossible, disastrous mouth, and this throbbing thing between us and all over me that I was afraid to name.

Jovi leaned in closer, until his face was so close to mine that I couldn't tell if he wanted to—

But he didn't.

I should have been *happy* he didn't.

He only watched me, even closer now. He smelled like pine and spice. And he was only more beautiful up close.

Jovi looked at me like I was a puzzle that needed solving, but I told myself that had to be a good thing, because I knew too many terrible men already and *they* only looked at me like I was meat.

He shifted slightly. His gaze moved all over my face.

I held my breath.

"Rux," he said, like my name was some kind of prayer. "Is something wrong with you? I mean this on a deep level. Your brain. Is it functional?"

"I...don't know how to answer that."

His mouth curved, but it was not a smile. "Why aren't you afraid?"

CHAPTER THREE

"I AM!" I REPLIED, STUNG. "Who wouldn't be afraid of a strange man in their room, no matter what he was there to do?"

I wanted to jerk back, away from him, but something stopped me. And I felt a little foolish, too. Was I really *upset* that my *executioner* was questioning my level of apprehension? I didn't think that spoke well of my mental health, if I was honest.

Just like the fact that I couldn't seem to stop noticing the spectacular beauty of his face, even under these circumstances.

Maybe there was something wrong with me.

I frowned. "Are you asking me if I'm...*mentally challenged*?"

Jovi didn't answer. Instead, he seemed to *inhale* me, and he took his time doing it. And then everything in me stuttered to a halt when he reached over and took my chin in his fingers.

Stuttered, then stopped, then *howled* back to life.

I felt every single cell of my body burst into flame. I could feel blisteringly hot color flood my cheeks. I could *feel* him, was the thing. I could feel him everywhere. His fingers were hard and faintly calloused, and I did not need to test the grip he had on me.

I knew perfectly well that I would not be able to move my face unless he let me.

But that thought didn't make me afraid. It only made me...hotter.

I was beginning to suspect that when it came to him, my challenges were not mental at all. I was beginning to understand that they were disastrously physical.

"You're nervous," he declared, those gleaming, unreadable, pitiless dark eyes all over my face. "But not afraid. And yet I think you know exactly who I am."

"I think I know what you do," I said, which wasn't quite an agreement.

His eyes narrowed. "Those are the same thing." He stayed there, holding my face still, and so I was still, too. "How interesting that you're quiet now, Rux. With my hand on you. Very interesting indeed. Have you made your choice?"

"What choice?" I asked, too hot and *strange* inside to track what he was saying, but then I remembered. "Oh. The gag. Or you're going to drug me."

He made a faint noise at the back of his throat, and I willed myself to come online. The way a normal woman would have, I was sure. To be horrified. Sickened straight through. To have adrenaline storming through me because of *fear*.

Because of what might happen next.

And it wasn't that I didn't have an overload of adrenaline.

But Jovi was right. I wasn't *afraid*.

He brushed a finger down the side of my neck. "I don't need drugs to knock you out. A simple blood choke will do the trick."

And when he kept moving that finger down the side of my neck, lazily, I learned more things about myself in that moment than anyone should have to know. Things I could never unlearn. Things I would always see in my mirror, I suspected.

Assuming I lived long enough to see my reflection again.

"But as you think about it," he continued in that same low voice while his finger paused, then retraced its firestorm path, "why don't you tell me why you are acting as if this is a date."

I wanted to argue that, but I couldn't. Because while I wouldn't have said that was what I was doing, it was very clear to me that my reactions were…not what they ought to have been.

I swallowed, hard. "What kind of life do you think I have?"

He moved his chin in such a way as to suggest a shrug. "I have given it no thought at all. Surely you know that you are nothing but a pawn in the games your father mistakenly thinks he can play."

"So you have given it some thought." I might have regretted saying that. I should have. But I was too mesmerized by Jovi himself. By that unearthly beauty of his face, which was not to say that I couldn't see the truth of him in the brutal symmetry of it. In the five-o'clock shadow that had taken over his jaw.

My tragedy was that the truth didn't make him less beautiful to me.

He inclined his head slightly. "I am aware of your position, that is all."

"They are the same thing," I said quietly, and I could tell he heard the echo of his own words. "My life is being a well-behaved pawn who causes my father no trouble. He's marrying me off. Everyone is pretending it is not an outright sale, but it is, of course. Unscrupulous men pretending that they can trust each other. One of them delivers a daughter who is nothing to him but a commodity. This makes an enemy something more like an ally, but that doesn't make the daughter in question safe, it makes her dependent on the health of that alliance." I shrugged. "But they will congratulate themselves at the wedding. They will smoke cigars, share a drink. Neither one of them will think of me as a person. Or at all, if we're honest. It's nothing but business."

Only after I said all that did I realize it was the first time I ever had.

I knew better than to say such things out loud in this house. And in the convent, where a great many men with questionable values sent the daughters they intended to use for their own purposes, we were allowed to speak only in designated areas, at designated times. Everything else was reserved for quiet contemplation and prayer.

Which was to say, we were only allowed to talk when we were supervised. Friendships were encouraged. Confidences—perish even the thought.

If I lived long enough to look back on this night from an analytical distance, it was entirely possible that I would be sad that I was a girl who found she could only communicate her intimate thoughts and feelings to a total stranger who, even worse, had come to do her harm.

But maybe there was a kind of liberation in the fact that all of that was unlikely.

It finally occurred to me that if people were going to hurt me anyway, I might as well speak my mind first.

Either way, I didn't stop.

"Anyway," I said quietly. "At least you're honest."

His gaze snapped back to mine, and held. "Always," he said. *"Per i miei peccati."*

I knew enough Italian to understand that. He was telling me he was honest to a fault. Somehow, I believed him.

"You're here to kill me," I said, quietly, and I wasn't sure where the strength came from to say that, either. Directly *to* him. I couldn't escape the strange feeling that it had something to do with him. That he was emboldening me. "You'll probably hurt me first. That's how this goes, generally speaking."

And then I was holding my breath again, as he held my gaze for a long moment—

Until, at last, he inclined his head. Just slightly.

"Okay, then." And despite my bravado, I could hear the shudder in me. It was right there, in my voice. "Why do we have to go somewhere else?"

"A blood choke it is," he replied.

His fingers moved to my neck again, and he leaned even closer, and for a moment I...did nothing.

My heart was going wild in my chest, but I really couldn't tell if that was fear coming in late, or the fact that he was hooking his other arm around me, almost as if he intended to—

"Gag," I said. Maybe loudly, upon consideration. "I want a gag."

He was so close now. Everything was that evergreen scent, something else like warmth beneath it, and that slow, intense way he turned his head to look straight at me.

Now he was closer to me than any other man ever had been.

Jovi stroked that finger down the length of my neck. "As you wish."

And there was another long, wild, impossible moment that seemed to stretch out across time—

But then he moved.

This time it was even more lyrical than when he stood still. And it was faster.

He reached behind me for my pillow. And as I found myself gasping for air, the feel of his hand at my throat and his arm over my shoulders seeming to drum in me like its own pulse—even though he'd let me go—he ripped off strips of fabric from the pillowcase. With his bare hands.

Then he was moving off the bed and pulling me with him so easily it made me feel something like silly.

To have imagined that I could have talked him into anything he didn't already wish to do. To have thought for even a moment that I could have done anything about the situation I found myself in. Anything at all.

Out of my bed, I found myself standing before him in my short-sleeve pajama set, complete with little shorts, which felt a great deal like a tactical error.

Jovi's dark gaze was cool, assessing. But his hands when they touched my skin were so hot it took my breath away.

He turned me around, easily. So very easily that it was as if I was as light and insubstantial as one of my down pillows, and something in me braced, assuming that he would rip me apart as easily.

But instead, I felt one big hand of his wrap around both of my wrists, and then he was tying them together into the small of my back. Snugly.

When that was done, I felt him kneel behind me. I glanced down, because there was something about his position. There was something about a big, scary man, sculpted and beautiful, kneeling there beside my bed with his hands on my body—

It took me long moments to realize that what he was doing was tying my ankles together, too.

He turned me around, but I was off-balance now. I found myself slumped back against the side of my high bed. My hands were bound, but reached out and gripped onto the coverlet behind me, as if that might ground me. That last little bit of something familiar.

Because the man standing in front of me was death. I knew it. I could see it.

What I couldn't understand was this simmering thing inside me that wanted to glory in that. In him.

Maybe it was what I'd been trying to tell him tonight—or explain to myself out loud while I was at it. All of the men my father had presented to me had death in their eyes. All of them were violent, brutal.

I didn't have to know anything about them to know this. It was obvious at a glance.

The fact that this one was also beautiful felt like a gift.

Then again, it was possible I was just looking to make a gift out of the usual shit show that was life as Boris Ardelean's daughter. Maybe it didn't really matter either way.

"Last chance," Jovi said in that cool, pitiless voice of his. Even with his warm accent, he sounded like what he was.

Deadly.

"To save myself?" I asked. "But without my hands or the use of my legs? I'm not sure what that would look like."

"I can put you to sleep, *baggiana*," he told me. Then he reached over and fitted his hand around my neck.

At first it was gentle. As if he was learning the shape of me and feeling my pulse in his palm. But then his grip tightened.

Just a little.

Then a little more.

Then more still, until I felt my mouth drop open, my breath escape me, and that ripe weighted softness between my legs *bloom* into a hectic kind of blaze.

"Then," he told me, his voice almost something like a croon, "you can cling to the notion that this is something that is happening to you only. And that you have no choices. That you are nothing at all but a hapless victim, caught up in the clutches of dangerous men."

"That's exactly what I am." But my chin lifted up of its own accord. "But I've come to terms with my lot in life. Do you really think I didn't expect to see you one of these days? You or someone like you. The angel of death at my bedside. One way or another, it was always going to be like this for me."

"It was always going to be ugly," he agreed, though when his fingers flexed against my throat—just enough to get my attention—I thought I'd hit a nerve. Somewhere in there, very deep. "But tonight, it turns out, it is me. And I have a different aesthetic than butchers like your father."

"Art is in the eye of the beholder," I managed to get out, that hand tight enough that I wasn't entirely certain he was going to let me keep breathing.

I wondered if this had been all an elaborate setup on his part, making it seem as if I would have more time when he knew if he would snuff me out, just like this. Making it seem like talking to him worked, or might work. Making it seem like this was anything other than what it was. The execution of an asset, to be used as leverage against a more important player.

Maybe what he really liked was toying with *hope*.

"Don't worry," I managed to squeak out. "I promise to give you an excellent review."

Once again, the dark ferocity in his gaze seemed to…thicken.

Jovi didn't squeeze his hand tighter. Instead, he let

go of my throat, and before I could truly process that, he was tying first one strip of ripped pillowcase over my mouth. He secured it tightly enough so that it pulled between my lips and made me have to think entirely too much about the placement of my tongue.

But he wasn't done. He took another strip and tied it over the first, this one wide enough to cover the lower part of my face entirely.

Then he stepped back, checked his work with a few quick jerks of his fingers, then moved back again—this time to cast his cool gaze around the room, letting it land on the bed.

"Now, I'm afraid, I need your blood." And I was sure that I saw something like a smile in his gaze when I jerked at that. "Calm yourself, Rux. I only require a little. We need to leave a message, you understand."

And I didn't know what he was going to do. What I knew was that I wanted to make the decision. This might be nothing more than false hope I was selling myself, this might be a farce all the way around—but if I chose it, it was mine.

This was the kind of mantra that had gotten me through my childhood. If I chose to talk back to my father—which could be anything from saying hello at the wrong time, or being *too much*, whatever that meant—if I chose the beating, it hurt less.

If I chose the things this man planned to do to me, then they were mine, too.

Or maybe I thought he might be as well.

So I nodded as if he was asking for my permission. I followed that up by jerking my head toward my bedside table where a very small nail kit lay open with a sharp pair of scissors readily at hand.

He followed my gaze, then looked back at me. "What a bossy thing you are, assuming a man like me does not come prepared. But this is even better."

And then he reached over and picked up the scissors. *My choice*, I told myself.

Then he turned back to me and hauled me up with one arm, tossing me face down onto the bed in a single, easy movement.

Everything inside me went still, then seemed to catapult off into the ether as he climbed onto the bed after me.

Then his hands were on me.

And before I could process that, I hissed at the sting of the pinprick I felt in one finger, grateful that he hadn't given me any warning—

Then less grateful as I felt that same prick in another finger and another. In all of them, one after the next, with relentless precision. I buried my face in the bed. I gave myself over to the inevitability. Then his hands were on my hands, pressing them in a way that didn't make sense until I thought about the fact that he wanted blood.

The stinging faded, and when it did, I could pay more attention to the position that I was in, on my bed with my ass in the air and my hands behind my back and him—

But he flipped me over, and looking at him was… worse.

And much, much better than any little bit of stinging.

Jovi's gaze was bright. Hot, I was sure of it.

But his voice was like ice when he said, "Roll."

I forgot I couldn't speak, but the noise I made must have indicated confusion.

"Roll around," he told me, the words a soft but implacable order. "Make a mess."

So that was what I did.

And it should have been sickening. It should have been creepy and strange, but that wasn't what it felt as I writhed about on the bed, spurred on by his merciless gaze. As I got too warm and my pajama top rode up and I could feel his gaze on the swath of my belly it showed him.

That wasn't what I felt as I flung myself this way and that, rolling and shaking myself over my sheets and the covers, and anything else I could touch my hands. I made myself *hot*. I made myself feel disheveled.

Inside and out.

And I could feel all of it throbbing between my legs, like he was branding me without even laying a finger upon me. With nothing more than that intent, hot gaze.

The first person in my entire life who had ever really seen me. All of me.

That notion made me shudder so hard it was like a terrible wave, a cramp and a rush and *almost*—

"Enough," he said, and I stopped, and didn't know why I felt a sort of sob roll through my chest, like loss. I swallowed it down.

I didn't know how long I'd been rolling around like that. A few moments? An hour? A whole lifetime? I couldn't tell.

Jovi moved toward me then and looked at me, almost curiously, as he pushed my hair back out of my face. I felt a moment of wonder and terrible shame that he could feel the damp heat of my skin.

That mouth of his curved again. Then he hauled me to the edge of the bed and bent me over it, so I was face down once more.

That wasn't better, either.

Nor was the way that he took his time sucking on each and every one of the fingertips he'd hurt.

Until I was...

I didn't know what I was. I didn't know what he was doing.

But it was more than just a wave. It was like a storm. It was terrible.

It was something very much *not terrible* at all. It was heat and suction and the wetness of his mouth, and I was remembering what his mouth looked like, that sensual impossibility—

My legs were pressed together, and I was already overstimulated, and my breasts were pressed down into the bed so I could feel my nipples drag against the mattress with every breath I took.

And I could feel a different storm beginning, deep between my legs, rolling and surging and growing and *almost*—

Once more with the *almost*—

But he pulled me up again then. He stood me beside the bed and when he looked down at my face, I had the impression that he was laughing.

Though of course he made no sound.

I couldn't bear to look at him with all the sensation careening around inside me, so I looked over at the bed instead. Something in me hitched, because I could see the blood everywhere. Not a lot, but enough to terrify anyone who came inside, I'd think. And the bed was a mess, the covers strewn all about and the pillow ripped and shredded, with feathers everywhere. Almost as if—

"You see it now," he said, much too close to my ear. "My vision. A present for your father from Il Serpente."

He didn't wait for me to react. Or maybe I had finally frozen in fear the way a normal person would have a long time ago—though there was not one part of me that thought this was *fear*, only that it should be.

The bed could look however it looked. I was the one who knew what had and hadn't happened there. I also knew that no one in this house would mourn me or what they would imagine had occurred here when they saw it.

The only thing my father would mourn was his bargaining power.

Somehow, that soothed me. Somehow, it made me more deeply appreciative of Jovi's *artistry*, such as it was.

He lifted me up then and tossed me over his shoulder as if, once again, I weighed no more than a single down feather.

And that left me all alone with the thoughts in my head as his shoulder pressed into my soft belly.

I could hold on to nothing as he moved. I had nothing to do but feel the faint ache in my fingertips, far outweighed by the sensation and memory of his mouth on each and every one of them. I had nothing but the memories of my reaction to his touch, the sure knowledge that he knew exactly what he had done to me.

So I did the only thing I could.

I shut my eyes and told myself the thing I always did.

This is my choice. This is what I want. I am getting exactly what I deserve.

And then he opened the door to my bedroom and stepped through it, into whenever waited for us outside.

Directly into the fate I'd *chosen*, so whatever happened, it was mine.

CHAPTER FOUR

JOVI MOVED QUICKLY and quietly, as always. The weight on his shoulder should have been unremarkable to him, and he told himself that was exactly what it was, because that was what it should have been.

But so far it appeared that nothing about this interaction with the disconcerting Rux Ardelean was *unremarkable*.

It took him the whole way down the isolated hallway of her father's little fortress, where her bedchamber sat apart from the rest of the house—a lot like her role in her family was similar to his role in his, an observation that he could not understand why he was making, as if he wished for some kind of *connection*—to realize why the sensations in him were so unusual.

It was a distraction. *She* was a distraction.

When Jovi had never been distracted, by anything, ever.

He was not certain he knew what to do in such extraordinary circumstances, so he concentrated on the usual things. The simple necessities that got him through a job, which in this case involved carrying his *wholly routine* cargo to the door at the end of the hall.

There he cast an assessing eye over the guards he'd carefully incapacitated on his way in.

Because he never killed unnecessarily. *Quality over quantity*, he had once told his uncle in his cousin's hearing. He lived by this.

The men were both still out and would come to, eventually, to find that they had terrible headaches. And likely far bigger problems than that when they had to explain their inability to do their jobs to a man like Boris Ardelean, who did not play by Jovi's rules.

But then, everyone had problems.

Jovi's included this appalling *awareness* he had of the woman over his shoulder. The way he could feel her body in a variety of concerning ways, when he shouldn't have given her a second thought. Yet he was entirely too clear on exactly where her breasts brushed against his back. And he couldn't seem to stop thinking about the fact that his hand was on the sweet curve of her ass as he held her in place.

These were details that should not have affected him one way or another.

Worse than that, he kept getting the scent of her in his nose, soaps and lotions and whatever else she used that made her smell the way sunshine felt. The taste of her blood in his mouth, a shimmery copper that made him wonder if vampires were onto something.

As if he was fanciful enough to believe in mythical creatures in the first place.

And beyond all that—all horrifying enough—there was the curious predicament of his heart.

Jovi could not recall ever thinking about his *heart* before. It was an organ. It beat. The end.

But tonight it seemed to have taken on a life of its own. It was as if when he'd put her fingers in his mouth, her blood had made his thicken. As if she'd infected him. Now his heart seemed swollen, tender.

And it beat far harder than it should.

So hard and so loud that he was surprised all the rest of the arms dealer's largely useless guards weren't summoned by the noise.

But they weren't.

Somehow, only he seemed to hear it, hammering away like it wanted out.

Once out of Rux's hallway and back in the main part of the house, he looked around. And stood still a moment, listening. Making sure that everything was as quiet as it had been when he'd slipped inside.

Only when he was certain it was did he methodically make his way through the house, down into the servants' quarters and out the side door that he paused to rearm from his mobile, because anything electronic could be hacked.

When the door was armed, he waited another moment and then moved quickly through the shadows of what was meant to be some kind of courtyard, timing it perfectly. Ardelean, convinced of his own importance, had a whole show of spotlights and barbed wire to announce his great significance to all of Czechia, yet had failed entirely to account for human error. In Jovi's experience, this was often the case with men who paid others to do what they would not do themselves.

Bought loyalty was merely betrayal in waiting.

In this case, Jovi walked out the way he'd walked in, through the unarmed door the servants used to sneak a smoke on duty.

He closed it tight behind him and walked quickly but without any urgency down the hillside until he reached the armed Range Rover he'd parked in the drive of a quiet house whose owners were abroad. Having backed in, he paused at the boot of the vehicle and listened once again. For footsteps. For dogs. For any hint that he'd tripped a security measure somewhere. But the little neighborhood of wannabe oligarchs on a Czech hill was sleepy in these predawn hours, and still.

He opened the hatch of the Range Rover and loaded Rux inside, waiting for her reaction—but once again, all she did was gaze at him with those sober gray eyes. And nod, as if she was extending him her permission.

That, too, made his heart catapult about in a way Jovi did not like.

Profoundly.

He secured her, but he also covered her with a blanket in a manner that he could only call considerate—*careful*, he corrected himself, he was only being *careful*, as befit the situation—and was perhaps a little too relieved to drive away.

He needed to remember himself. He needed to regain his bearings.

That he had never once forgotten himself or lost his bearings before was something he could interrogate and explore once this was finished.

Tonight was a show for an audience of one, who

would react predictably to this demonstration that his power was a joke, and Jovi thought he'd set the scene beautifully.

The first act of the play that was about to unfold required specific extra inducements. Just to make certain things clear to a man like Ardelean who had dared reach so far above himself.

A man who truly believed he alone could stand against Il Serpente.

Nowhere was safe. Nothing was off-limits. There were no guards and no security measures that could keep him safe. His own home had been invaded while he slept nearby. The state of Rux's bedroom would indicate that Ardelean had no idea what happened under his roof, or for how long, or to what end.

For a man who considered himself an unassailable king, this would be unsupportable.

It would drive him mad.

And Jovi knew men like this all too well. Ardelean didn't have to give one shit about his daughter to lose it over what something like this represented.

Jovi drove through the early morning streets of Prague efficiently. He did not speed or crawl. There was absolutely nothing worth noticing about the vehicle he drove or the way he drove it, aside from the fact that it was bulletproof, suggesting that he was expecting to be fired upon.

He fully expected Ardelean to access Prague's CCTV. And when the cameras were played back to find the registration number of the Range Rover, it would, of course be false. And he had a particular blurry tint on the windows of this vehicle that would keep the Policie České Republiky from making his life difficult, but he'd made certain to let Boris Ardelean's personal cameras catch his face.

The real pictures of him would be there for Boris Ardelean to see once he understood his daughter had been taken.

Antonio wanted the man to know exactly who had come for him. Who could have walked directly into Boris's room, if he'd wished, but had not. Who had instead wandered about Boris's house as if he owned it and helped himself to a little treat on the way out.

What Antonio really wanted was respect, but fear would do.

Jovi wound his way through the ancient city and then on into one of its less tourist-friendly neighborhoods. He found the house in question, opened its gates with the remote app on his mobile, and backed into its garage.

Only when the garage door was closed did he turn the engine off, then exit the vehicle so he could attend to his passenger. When he opened the hatch, Rux was curled up right where he'd left her beneath her blanket. And her eyes were open, so there was no escaping the immediate blast of her curiously direct slate gray eyes.

Jovi could not comprehend why everything about handling this woman was different. He had spent his whole life adhering to certain protocols, the number one of which was to never, ever personalize these experiences. He never had.

If asked—and Carlo had certainly asked him—he

said he had never seen the need to personalize anything.

One more thing his cousin hated about him. If Jovi had cared that his cousin thought he was a freak, that would be the kind of personalization he didn't do. He didn't. He'd only shrugged.

This was why he was so good at what he did. This was why his uncle kept him alive.

And yet Rux defied every last protocol.

Or maybe he was the one who was defying them, because he was the one who reached out and untied her ankles first, rubbing them briskly with his hands, in case she'd gone numb. Her skin was cooler than it had been in her bedroom, even with the blanket, and he didn't like that. It made his treacherous heart…react.

He reached behind her to untie her hands, too, rubbing them in the same matter-of-fact manner. And then, even as she made a noise in the back of her throat, he took his time pulling her forward until she was sitting on the lip of the bumper. He checked her hands, making sure that the tiny pinpricks he'd put in her fingers were no longer bleeding and that her skin was not turning blue.

When he was satisfied, he released her so he could take the gag out of her mouth, too.

And it was only when he cupped her chin and rubbed his thumb over her lips—an urge he did not understand—and then pressed it between them so she almost had no choice but to suck on it—he understood this even less—did it truly dawn on Jovi what he was doing.

Not that it stopped him.

Gray eyes met his, widened in something far smokier than simple shock, and then it was her turn to suck.

The way he had in her bedroom, learning each of her fingers. She sucked on him, and he felt her tongue move over his thumb, and slowly, the dryness of her mouth abated.

He told himself that had been his only aim.

But there were other distractions when he pulled his thumb back, and then, with a swift glance at the concrete garage, swept her up into his arms.

Rux looked startled, but she slid an arm around his neck. And then he was carrying her into the house, for all intents and purposes a parody of a romantic clinch.

He could not account for the effect this one had on him. He would have considered her a sorceress or this some kind of witchcraft—but he believed in neither.

The consequences of real life were too dire and impossible to escape. What little magic he'd ever known had died out, long ago.

Jovi almost stopped short at that, because he never thought about such things on the job.

He tried not to think of such things at all.

But he kept carrying her, taking her up the narrow stairs and then into the first room they encountered.

Inside there was nothing but a sturdy chair. It sat in the center of the tiled room, and above it, two thin wires were bolted to the ceiling. At the end of them were leather cuffs.

"If you feel you must relieve yourself, the bathroom is through there," he told her, and nodded at the door on the other side of the room. He did not need to go and check it, because he already knew there was nothing inside that she could use as a weapon, to hurt him or herself. The window was boarded over and bolted shut.

"Such courtesy," Rux murmured as he set her bare feet on the ground. "You are truly the consummate host, Jovi."

The part of him that wanted to punish such flippancy was overruled by the part of him that couldn't believe she talked to him as if he... She wasn't afraid of him at all.

As if he wasn't a monster.

He thought he felt a rib crack.

She disappeared inside the bathroom and he tried to empty himself of all these odd thoughts and impulses, all this noise and clamor. He preferred stillness. He preferred solitude. He preferred a true emptiness within—

But instead he heard the toilet flush. Then the running taps. And then, inevitably, the low rattle that told him she was trying to pry open the window.

He decided he wouldn't have respected her much if she hadn't made an attempt.

When she opened the door again, she paused in the doorway. "What a remarkably scoured-clean and sanitized bathroom," she said brightly. "It looks like it's never been used by a human."

He indicated the chair before him with a jut of his chin. Rux walked toward him, his ribs sustaining damage as his heart went wild, and Jovi had to accept that the unthinkable had really and truly happened.

She was getting to him.

She already had, when in his whole life, attractive women had been nothing but interchangeable. There were too many, there were always more, and they flitted about his family like so many foolish moths to an open flame. *An endlessly renewable resource*, his uncle liked to declare.

Jovi had never allowed himself to be distracted.

But there was something about Rux that made his bones suddenly seem to sit wrong inside his body.

There were those clever eyes in that serious shade of gray, particularly notable in such a pretty face. There was all that glossy dark hair that made her look moody and mysterious, and made him want to bury his hands in it to see if it felt as good as he thought it would, like raw silk. There were her cheekbones that made him want to trace them with his mouth. And there was *her* mouth that hinted at an overbite and now made him think about the way she'd closed her lips around his thumb and sucked him in deep.

He had the disturbing and unwelcome realization that he was attracted to *her*. Specifically. Not because she was a very pretty woman by any measure, but because she was Rux.

If he had been anywhere else, doing anything other than this, he was certain this revelation would have made him leave. At once. And never return.

But she drew closer and there was that scent again. Flowers, perhaps. Something sweeter, like dark brown sugar. He watched as she obediently sat in the chair and found himself looking more closely at what she was wearing.

Pajamas, that was all. They should have been unremarkable right along with everything else, but like everything else, they were...not.

The trouble was, he'd seen them on her as she'd writhed about on that bed. He'd seen the swell of her belly and the hint of all that smooth skin. And he'd seen the lower curve of her ass when he'd bent her over the bed, and when he'd laid her face down to work on those fingers.

He'd seen too much, that was clear.

And he'd been paying attention to the parts of *her* that he'd seen instead of the pattern on the pajamas themselves. Jovi frowned now as he made out the tiny little evergreen trees, festooned in Christmas colors, all over the smooth cotton fabric.

"Christmas was last month," he said darkly, as if she had perhaps gotten confused.

"I wanted to feel festive," she replied in that way of hers that managed to be insolent and intriguing all at once. "And behold my success. This certainly seems like a party, doesn't it?"

He moved closer, stepping between her legs so he could reach up and pull one cuff down, then the other, fastening each around her slender wrists in a way that could not be undone with one hand. The movements were like breathing to him, all muscle memory and no conscious thought.

But now when he breathed, he breathed in her scent. And he wondered about that flush on her cheeks, what it meant and whether or not it extended into softer, sweeter places. And he was putting together a fairly detailed mental schematic of the precise size and shape of those breasts he'd felt flush against his back—

It wasn't only his heart that was going rogue, Jovi realized then.

His cock was so hard it, too, hurt.

Never before in all of his life had he ever confused work with play.

Rux was getting to him in ways he could not understand.

He did not *want* to understand.

She was secured. It didn't matter what *feelings* were assaulting him—all that mattered was that simple truth. She was secured, as intended, and he underscored that by stepping back, crossing his arms over his chest, and gazing down at her as impassively as possible.

Maybe he was proving to himself that he could.

A thought that made him feel—

He stopped himself right there and reminded himself who the fuck he was. Then did his best to act like it.

As if he was still the man who hadn't felt his own heartbeat in longer than he could recall.

He watched as she tested the cuffs, and, again, understood that something in him respected that. Only a fool accepted that a door was locked without testing it himself.

When she was finished, she let her arms hang so that the wires held them aloft instead of fighting against them, he found that interesting, too. Once again, Rux seemed more relaxed than he would have expected. More relaxed than most could have been, given her predicament. Certainly more relaxed than any other person he'd had in a position like this.

But the last time he'd asked her why she wasn't afraid, it had changed something in him. It had fundamentally altered something in him that he couldn't name, but he could still *feel* it, like one of those hangovers his cousins joked about.

Jovi had never experienced one of those, either. His entire life was about maintaining control and wielding it in service of his uncle.

And here he was, standing in a bare, stripped-down room where he held every last scrap of power there was. Where he controlled every single thing that had happened or could happen.

There was no reason that he should feel *drunk*, or what he assumed drunk must feel like, having witnessed it so many times in others.

He thrust that aside.

"Now we will decide how much of an actress you are," he said in a forbidding voice—his usual voice, he corrected himself. "I will take a video. In it, you will beg and plead for your father to save you."

He expected her to burst into tears, but instead, she laughed.

Perhaps he should have expected that, he thought. Most people were so terrified of him they did whatever he asked, but Rux had already proved that was not her.

"That's a colossal waste of time," she told him.

"I beg your pardon?"

"He wouldn't care. That's the point, right? To get

him to care? To make him feel badly about something? *Anything?*"

"The point is to impress upon him that his own child is suffering for his decisions," Jovi said. Repressively.

But she only laughed again, this time jangling the wires enough that they swung and made noise. "What makes you think that would bother him?"

Jovi gazed down at her. "Of course it would bother him."

It would, he was quite certain, offend the man on every level, since he seemed to think himself the master of all he surveyed. This would take the message left behind in Rux's bedroom and underscore it.

"No," Rux said, quietly, and there was something so grave in her gaze. "It won't bother him. He doesn't care if I'm hurt. I suppose that he might be enraged that I'll fetch a lower price, or be taken off the market entirely, because that would affect his bottom line." She did not seem upset when she said this. There was no resignation, no hint of pain. She sounded *certain*, that was all, and it was the kind of certainty that took years to reach this level of calm. "My father has more emotional attachment to the packages he has delivered."

It wasn't only that she was saying these things. Certainly, Jovi had met others in the course of the work he performed for his uncle who went out of their way to make it clear that they were not a strategic source of pressure against anyone, especially not the given target.

But none had ever stated it so matter-of-factly. Or while laughing.

In point of fact, Jovi could not recall very many people laughing in his presence, ever.

He had always assumed that was because they all knew what he did. What he was—a monster on a leash.

What did not make sense was that he knew Rux was aware of this, too. She'd known exactly what he was the first moment she'd seen him. And still she laughed.

She laughed again now. "Besides," she said, sounding something more like rueful, "I will never beg him and I do not cry. I would rather die than let him see me so diminished."

It reminded him of his mother's brief defiance on that terrible night, her attempt to fight the inevitable—

But he did not think about his mother. He did not think about that night. He certainly did not equate these people he met because of his job with his lost family, because that would make him—

Something inside Jovi cracked at that and he had the strangest notion that it was his ribs. The ribs that should have been holding that wild heart of his in place. That wild, excessively beating heart seemed to know things about him—about her—that he did not.

It made him furious.

He blamed her for that, too, because it was another fucking *feeling*. He never, ever, bothered with those.

He never had to bother with those because he never felt them in the first place.

But nothing about this had been right, not since the first moment she'd lifted her gaze from that book of hers and fixed it on him.

The parallels to his mother were bad enough, but

that wasn't all it was. It was a one-two punch of unwanted memories and something else.

And he had told her he was honest, so he was honest with himself, too.

The truth was that he wanted her. That he had never wanted anything else, not in any of his life that he could remember—and he had locked that other part of himself away. He had hidden it. It was as dead as his family was, and it told him something he didn't want to know about himself that he used that word to describe the traitor Donatello and the necessary casualties of the choices he'd made.

Jovi *wanted*.

And he knew better than anyone else that if he gave in to that, the price would be unbearable.

"Did you hear me?" she asked, and he wondered what she saw in his face.

Because he knew, somehow, that in addition to all of her other offenses tonight, she was the only one who had ever managed to read him.

It was another hint that all of this would end in despair.

"I told you that I would rather die," Rux said again, with a little more heat behind it. "And I mean it."

"Luckily, you foolish woman," Jovi growled back at her, "that is the point of this entire exercise."

CHAPTER FIVE

AN EXCELLENT CURE for my bravado, it turned out, was being hogtied, thrown in the back of a thankfully swanky Range Rover, and then chained up in a room that looked…exactly the way a room like this always looked in every version of it I'd ever seen on television.

I told myself to be happy it wasn't a serial killer's basement or a run-of-the-mill warehouse in a conveniently abandoned industrial estate.

I would have preferred that strange heat again. That heart-poundingly close call with the wild, rising wave inside me that he had seemed to control so easily.

That he had managed to rouse and then deny, twice.

My mouth was dry again now, but still not from fear. "I don't actually know if you mean that literally."

"I think, Rux, that you know I do."

But something happened to him, too. Right there in front of me as I watched.

I could see it like another sort of wave, crashing over him and evident to me in the way his dark eyes flashed that molten gold. And the way his impossible mouth tightened.

Now that we were past the intrusion into my bedroom and the whole kidnapping escapade—which had been both much less traumatic and a bit more uncomfortable than expected, because I hadn't felt the terror I should have but I really did not enjoy the pins and needles in my hands or the fabric of that gag against my tongue—I really tried to take him in.

I tried to really *see* this man who had done the thing I'd never managed to do and gotten me out of my father's clutches.

The typical kidnapper of my imagination, a common boogeyman for children raised with guards the way I had been, always wore dramatic stocking caps to announce their intentions from afar. They were always in head-to-toe black, might or might not sport the proverbial moustache, and could easily be confused for a cat burglar.

Or a cartoon.

Jovi was not wearing any of that. Jovi was wearing a crisp and perfectly tailored suit that had obviously been lovingly and exquisitely tailored to his precise and singular physique. He looked like he ought to have been wandering about Milan with a pack of fashion photographers in his wake. Or perhaps on a film set somewhere suitably sophisticated, all hushed wealth and abundance. There was nothing about him that suggested he was the sort of thug who abducted young women—other than the fact that he was a man, of course, and statistics suggested they were the ones out doing these things.

I doubted there were a lot of women who went about collecting girls like me for fun and profit.

The thing about Jovi was that he was beautiful here, too, in this secluded house. In this carefully empty room with only that secured window to suggest there was anything outside anyway.

But he wasn't *only* beautiful. Not even up close like this, where I suspected I could scream all I wanted to no avail—the way I hadn't even thought to do back home. There was that seething, brutal masculinity mixed in with all that perfection that somehow made not just his features seem less pretty and more formidable than they should have been, but made the inarguably elegant suit he wore the same.

Another man might have looked too *done*. Too manicured.

On Jovi, it was simply another indication that he was as deadly as he was beautiful. It was all part and parcel of the same package.

And looking at him made all of the heat in my body sink deep between my legs, then *hum*.

More than what he wore and how he behaved, it was clear that he was refined. Educated. Sophisticated in ways I could only imagine, given the confines I'd always lived in. There could not have been a greater contrast between my father and a man like this. My father, who considered himself all of those things, but was not. Boris Ardelean was nothing but a bully, thuggish and cruel. A bully with too much money and a deep and abiding disdain for the lives of others.

Jovi, on the other hand, was something far more dangerous than a *bully*.

For one thing, I doubted very much that it was

money that motivated him the way it did my father, even though it was clear to me that he had more than enough of it. He also wore his beautiful clothing too carelessly for him to have had to scrape and budget to earn them.

And now, whatever it was that was happening inside him—and maybe I was just making that up to make myself feel better, no matter what I thought I'd seen—he was staring at me so impassively that it made me stop breathing.

I blew out what air was left in my lungs to get myself started again, and I thought a little harder about what I felt. What this was. What was likely to happen.

I thought it all through and I still wanted it to be my choice. That was the main thing.

It was the only thing.

"Okay," I told him. "I'd like to die well, Jovi." I could see that hit him, and hard. It was like an electric bolt, and I could feel it as much in me as I could see it in him. "Maybe no one will ever know, but I think I will, somehow. And I think it matters."

His gaze went frigid for a moment. Then it *blazed*.

"You're a fool," he belted out at me, no hint of all that ice and control and *stillness*. "Death is death. Good, bad, indifferent. Nobody cares, nobody will remember you, and all of us will turn to worm food in the end."

"Thank you," I managed to say. "That's a lovely rendition of the last rites. Ashes to ashes. Dust to dust. One big circle, leading us ceaselessly back into the past—though I don't think that's quite the right quote—"

"Death is death, Rux." His voice was dark. Grim.

His eyes were on fire. "You might want to think about taking yours seriously."

He was right. I should. Then again, maybe I was.

My throat was dry again, and not because of ripped shreds from my pillowcases. I could still feel that thumb of his in my mouth, pressing into me, somehow beautiful when I knew it shouldn't have been.

But the real truth was that it had been one of most exciting things that had ever happened to me, and all of the other ones had happened tonight, too.

One after the next.

And no, I wasn't *mentally challenged* as previously accused. This was simply the reality of it all. He was the most excitement I'd ever encountered and that would have been true even if he wasn't gorgeous beyond measure.

But he was.

He really was.

"I'm taking this all very seriously," I assured him, and I tried my best to sound as calm and collected as possible, given the circumstances. "It's just that I think it would all be a little bit sadder and more heavy hitting if I had any kind of a life leading up to this moment, but I really didn't." Some inkling came to me at that, and I studied him. His stern expression. His stiff posture. Those unfathomable eyes. "Did you? *Do* you?"

He blinked, and on another person, that wouldn't even have been noticeable. But this was Jovi. This was a man who was so still he could teach stone how to settle.

That blink echoed in me like a revolution, so I didn't

want to pay too much attention to it. I didn't want him to hide it if it happened again.

What I wanted was for him to keep looking at me the way he was doing now, with fire everywhere and that answering kick of flame inside me. Because I had the strangest notion that these last moments of my life were the first and only ones I was actually *living*.

That all the rest of it had been empty pantomime on my father's nasty little stage, but this was the real thing.

Life was supposed to be messy. It was supposed to contradict and complicate, hurt and leave marks.

I'd read about these things.

But until tonight, I'd never experienced them.

I decided that it wasn't the strangest thing in the world that I wanted more. As much as I could get before it ended. It didn't make me broken or questionable or any of the other things people would say if they could look into this room and see us like this.

It made me a whole grown woman, not the little doll my father and his cronies had been bickering over for the past few years. It made me *alive*.

"What do you think having a life means?" Jovi frowned at me, but I took that like a victory. Any change in him was a triumph.

Anything that reminded me that this was a man, not a sculpture.

Or at least, that's what he was for me.

I wanted to believe that he had the same catastrophically intense reaction to me as I did to him.

Okay, I already believed it.

"Having a life is not being locked up in convents

or my father's house," I told him, sitting up a little straighter. "It's...being able to walk down any avenue in any city I fancy, and doing as I please as I go. Being able to eat what I want, when I want, and have to explain myself to no one. Not having to ask for permission or forgiveness for what I wear or think or say. To make some money that is only mine and spend it as I like. Is that so hard to imagine? To me it seems quite simple."

"This is what you're missing?"

There was something wrong about the way he asked that, I thought. It resonated in me, jagged and sharp.

He moved closer, so that once again he was nearly standing between my knees, and I had to tilt my head back and look far, far up the length of his torso to see his face.

I thought he would reach out to take my chin in his hand once more, or something like it—

But he didn't.

And the fact that he didn't make me feel something perilously close to *undone*.

"What small, insignificant things these are to bother wanting, *baggiana*." He sounded particularly dark and I felt my cheeks go hot, as if I'd exposed myself. "Where is it you think that people are living these uncomplicated lives you imagine are so fulfilling? I have been everywhere, and I will tell you, they do not exist, these lives."

I could not pull my gaze away from him. "They must."

"They cannot, because *people* are not simple," he

argued, that dark gaze seeming to wind its way *inside* me as he gazed down at me. "People are desperate and complicated, wicked and grasping."

"Is that what you are?" I asked him, and it felt like the most dangerous question I could possibly have dared utter.

Jovi shook his head, and for a moment I thought he looked like he was in pain.

"Most people scuttle about this planet, imagining that the things they do make some kind of difference. That they matter. Their petty feuds, their heartbreaks, their daydreams about futures they will never make real." He bent down and this time, when he smoothed his hand over my jaw, he kept going. He speared his long, elegant fingers into my hair, then used it to tug my head back. "But you and I, we know different, do we not?"

That didn't seem like a question he wanted the answer to, and that was a good thing, since the most I could do was stutter out a breath.

"You and I know that all of it is futile," he told me in that low, dark, rumbling voice of his that I could feel take up residence behind my ribs. "The bright, happy, pointless lives of people who are nothing more than prey. Just as you and I know that the world is sharply divided, is it not? Life belongs to the predator. Prey lives only insofar as predators allow it, and we both know that more often, they die."

"I've always heard that Italians are poetic," I murmured, and his grip in my hair was tight. It should have hurt.

Maybe it did hurt, but that, too, was *sensation*—and it turned out I was a glutton for every last scrap of sensation that I could hoard. That I could *feel* when for as long as I could remember, there had been so little but boredom, apprehension, and the inevitability of my own surrender. The tedium of the chokehold of the life my father allowed me, in the convent or under his disapproving eye. The endless stretch of these prison days without number.

I had no reason to think that marrying one of my father's cronies would be any different. Aside from the marital expectations, that Katarzyna had made certain to tell me were far better tolerated with wine. Or anything else I could get my hands on.

Because there are always dynastic expectations, she had said in her matter-of-fact way.

I don't know that I want to do any of those things, I had replied. *I don't like anyone who does.*

She had lifted her wineglass in my direction. *It is as my mother always said about giving birth*, she replied coolly. *Yes, of course, a woman* can *do it naturally, as women have done since the dawn of time, but why should she?*

"If I were you," Jovi told me in that forbidding way of his, undercut—or perhaps enhanced—by that electricity I could feel crashing all around him like an incoming storm, "I would be grateful that you do not have to live out the rest of your life as some plastic representation of a rich man's trophy. Pretending you do not know exactly how dark the shadows are all around you. All the blood and pain tied to every single moment that bores you."

"I have already lived that life," I reminded him. "As a rich man's daughter instead of his wife. I'm not sure it's any better."

"You and I do not get to have these blameless, anodyne years you speak of. Wandering down city streets, thinking we might read a newspaper in a café or while away an afternoon over a cribbage board." He laughed. It was a harsh, aching sort of sound. "This is not reality, Rux. Not for monsters like us, raised by demons and devils to suit their own ends. We don't get to be silly and dream of happy things. The moment you were born, your destiny was set. I am no different. The only difference between the two of us is that I accept what I am and what that makes me."

"But why did you accept it?" I asked, only understanding the urgency in the question when I could hear it hang between us. "What would happen if you refused to accept it?"

Jovi let go of me then, looking down at me as if he couldn't believe I'd asked him the question. As if I'd reached into his chest and ripped out his heart. I was half convinced that if I looked up at one of my chained, dangling hands, I'd see it there. Bright and red in the middle of this otherwise colorless room.

"Tell me one thing you think you've missed out on," he growled at me. "One thing that you imagine life would have given you if you'd been a happy little sheep, halfway to her own slaughter, like everyone else out there."

And I knew the answer immediately. I could feel it in my mouth, as surely as when he had pressed his thumb there.

"There are a lot of things," I told him. "There's a reason they say ignorance is bliss. I think they're right."

"No one who says such a thing is ignorant. They only fantasize that if they were, they would like it. But if that were true, everyone would be ignorant. Eve would never have tasted that apple." He shook his head. "One thing, Rux."

"I always thought I'd like to be kissed before I died," I said, because I couldn't seem to stop myself. "It seems a shame that never happened."

It seemed like a lot more than a shame.

But once I said it, the silence became deafening. So loud that it seemed to press in from all sides, a clamor beyond reason.

The look in his eyes was the same.

But I didn't back down. I looked straight at him, and I didn't let myself look away. I reminded myself that all I had in this life were the choices I made with what little time I had left.

So I tipped my head back and I didn't look away.

And I chose.

"The least you could do," I said quietly, "the very least, Jovi, is kiss me before you kill me. Don't you think?"

CHAPTER SIX

FOR A MOMENT, I thought the silence between us was so loud that he didn't actually hear me. That he was lost, too, in the ringing that was in my ears and the hammering in my chest. Maybe he could even feel the way my pulse was taking on a drumming all its own.

Maybe I'd only imagined I'd said such a thing.

And maybe, I tried to reason with myself, I should be happy if that was the case. I'd read enough to know that it wasn't exactly a healthy thing to imprint on the first stranger who came around, especially when he'd been sent to take me out as a message to my father. I didn't have to read anything to understand that my attraction to Jovi was bad enough, but that this dawning belief that deep down, he and I were the same—

That wasn't *mentally challenged*. That was straight up *unhinged*.

I'd been saved from my own worst impulses, I decided.

"Jovi," I began, "the thing about—"

But I never finished that sentence.

Because he made a sound that I'd never heard before. It was deep and low. Animal.

It seemed to pour out of his skin, as if his bones were making their own kind of music in the only way they knew how. It was everywhere, a wilder sound than the ringing in my ears or that slamming heartbeat that I was surprised hadn't catapulted me off the chair.

I heard it, I felt it, but more than that, I recognized it. *I knew it.* It was there, deep inside me, as if it had always been there. As if I had been made long ago to echo this thing in him.

That it only took meeting him. And now we could sing it out together.

That this was our song.

And we were made to sing it, just like this.

I knew this with every last cell in my body.

I thought he did, too. I was sure of it.

There was that look all over his beautiful face, that startled, astonished *recognition* that I could feel all over me. And deep inside me, too.

Jovi surged forward and took my face in his hands, lifting me up out of the chair and straight on up to my toes as his mouth covered mine.

I had never gone anywhere so willingly.

And the last rational thought I had was that I had truly never felt anything at all before this moment. Not one stray emotion. Not the faintest sensation.

Because *this* was everything.

It was every light, every color, every shade imaginable.

It was better than any song I'd ever heard or ever would.

And it was texture and need, swirling through me

with a force that might have scared me a little if I wasn't as wild for him as he was for me.

I could *feel* how much he wanted me.

It was the way he held me. It was the way he moved closer, pressing himself against me so I could return the favor. It was the urgency I could feel in every part of his body, mirroring mine.

Besides all this, his mouth was hard and demanding, stunning and *perfect*, and there was nothing the slightest bit tentative about the way he kissed me.

He kissed me the way he moved, lyrical and dangerous, deadly in every regard.

I wanted to put my arms around his neck, but I couldn't. The chains prevented it and there was something about that restriction that made me surge against him even more, with a wildfire intensifying within me. Deep between my legs, I was *alight*.

Because this time, I could feel all those things I'd felt while face down on my bed, but it wasn't the coverlet beneath me now. This time I was pressing my breasts against the wall of his chest. This time I was finally getting drunk on the taste of him, finally understanding how the world could spin away and disappear, leaving only the way he licked into me and taught me how to do the same to him.

And it seemed to me that I was made for nothing at all save this.

If he pulled back and told me so, I would have believed him.

As if he was the flint and I was the match, and I was rubbing myself against him, desperate for that spark.

Yet I couldn't think critically about that, or how to achieve it, or anything at all but the way he kissed me.

It was dirty. It was *fantastic*. He ate at my mouth, his hands moving my head where he wanted it, finding new angles, new fires, new ways to wreck us both. Everything was that dark, delirious heat, And nothing was neat or precise.

Nothing was *cold*.

We were scalding hot and burning brighter the longer it went on.

I wanted to kiss him forever.

I wanted to break free of the chains holding me and the ones I'd been locked in all my life and wrap myself around him. I wanted *him* with so much ferocity and certainty that I understood, at last, that I'd never *truly* wanted anything else in all my life.

He taught me how to kiss and how to yearn, all at once.

I could feel it everywhere. I could feel him like every slide of his tongue against mine was another way we were becoming one. As if we were *melting* into each other.

I could feel this in the breasts I rubbed against him, even in the hands that could not touch him. I could feel it wind all the way around me, and burrow deep into me, and I understood that whatever happened between us back in my father's house had been nothing more than gazing at an abyss through a safety glass.

This was something else.

This was a free fall.

There was nothing safe about *this*—about *him*—at all.

And I found it exhilarating. Magical.

Perfect.

Like I'd finally found my purpose.

His hands moved from my face to my neck, and I thought he was heading toward that choke he'd played with before. And I also thought…it would be all right.

If it happened now, it would be worth it.

But instead, Jovi pulled back.

He set me away from him, and the look on his face then was so ferocious that it made my legs feel weak—or perhaps it was just that he was the only thing holding me up.

Either way, I was something like grateful when I fell back down to take my seat in that chair. I expected him to thunder at me, do something terrible, or leave.

When he did none of the above, I decided I had no choice.

No choice but to honor all the terrible and wonderful and complicated things I could feel chasing around inside me. Because I really thought that despite his attempt to look as stone-faced as ever, what he actually looked like was shaken.

I knew that I was, and everything that had just happened suggested to me that he and I were more alike than not.

But I knew something else, too.

"Whatever you might think about the quality of life other people have, people who don't live in our world," I told him, my voice as measured as it could be when my mouth no longer felt like mine, "I haven't lived in either one. No fake security. Just the cages my father set out for me. I've never felt more alive than I have tonight, Jovi. I didn't know it was possible."

He was so still then. So still, and yet I was sure that I could see that fire still hot and wild in his gaze.

I could still feel it burning in me.

"It seems like a waste," I confessed. "To live twenty-two years but only really be alive for a few hours of one night." And now the taste of him in my mouth was the only thing that I could think about. The taste of him and the memory of his tongue moving on mine. The way he held me so tight and the way he made the kiss go on and on and on. "Tell me something, Jovi. What do I have to do to live?"

But that wasn't really what I wanted. I didn't want him to set me free on some shady boulevard in some city I'd only read about. I wanted a very specific life with whatever time I had left. So I decided I had to ask for it directly, because this was no time for playing games with the things I really wanted. I might not get the chance to ask again.

I took a breath. "What do I have to do to live a little longer...*with you*?"

I watched him take a breath, and in such a rough way that I was immediately conscious of the fact that until that moment, I hadn't actually seen him do anything so human and relatable as *breathe*. It was part of what made him so still, so scary.

I felt something in me shudder that here, now, he wasn't the stone sculpture he'd been when I met him.

"There's nothing you can do," he gritted out at me, but there was something in his gaze—some kind of tortured longing—that told me otherwise.

"There must be something," I argued, filled with a certainty that I knew didn't make sense. But what I did know was this *thing* between us was extraordinary. If it wasn't, he wouldn't react to it the way he did. *He* didn't live in the same cage I did. *He* would know better, surely. Yet here he stood, so I kept going. "Didn't you tell me everyone is wicked and compromised? Surely that means you, too."

There was something stark in his gaze. His face suddenly looked ravaged. "I am a man of vows." But he said it like those vows hurt him. Like they were tearing him apart where he stood. "I can kill you, and I will."

If I expected that to be the end of it, if I thought that he would do what he had been threatening—and hopefully fast—he didn't.

Instead, he stayed there, gazing at me in that same raw and savage manner, then turned around and left me there in that empty room.

With nothing but the heat inside me to keep me company.

But I could hear him close the door behind him as he went. The way I hadn't been able to hear any of the doors close behind us as we left my father's house, a lot like there was more force behind it this time.

A lot like he was feeling exactly the same way I was.

I could admit that was satisfying.

Because I was pretty sure I'd just witnessed the Jovi

version of storming off and slamming the door behind him.

Nothing could ever convince me that he hadn't felt that kiss the same way I had.

That we weren't both equally destroyed by it.

The only difference was, I wanted more. And while I suspected he might, too, he had *vows*.

It occurred to me then that he might have meant a specific set of vows. Marriage vows.

Something in me revolted, instantly. I didn't believe it. I couldn't. This thing roaring between us was too—

But.

But.

How many of my father's associates bragged openly about their many mistresses when their wives weren't in the room? Men like Jovi—

Again, something in me surged up in denial. I couldn't believe there were men like Jovi. I couldn't believe it was possible.

Still, the men in this world thought nothing of tramping all over their marriage vows. If anything, they took pride in it. They thought it was only their due.

Jovi's restraint was what set him apart from them.

And as I sat there, his taste in my mouth, I tried to force myself to face the reality of my situation. Finally.

I thought about my mother and what I liked to believe was her bid for freedom. I imagined her in some far-off city, maybe somewhere glamorous like Buenos Aires, listening to tango music and dancing her heart out on cobblestone streets. If I closed my eyes, I could see it. I could see her, smiling the way I doubted she'd had much call to do in her real life.

But the far greater likelihood was that she'd either been run off that road by my father's men, or they'd set it up to look that way because they didn't want anyone seeing how she'd *actually* died.

That sat in me. For a long while.

I had no sense of time, there in that room. In that way, it reminded me of the convent. And if I considered it the convent, it was really no scarier. I had spent a great many years sitting and kneeling in uncomfortable positions, carrying on conversations the only way I was permitted to. With myself. In my head.

Where everyone else had apparently found God, but I never had.

I couldn't allow myself to believe in a God who permitted a man like my father to prosper.

I blew out a breath now and leaned my weight forward, into my cuffs, because it felt good to stretch. I wasn't exactly warm, with my bare feet on the tile floor, but I didn't mind it. I could feel exhaustion rolling in, a reaction both to the adrenaline of all this and the fact I'd already been up late when Jovi had appeared in my bedroom. The cold floor was good. Years of having to get up at all hours for various prayers, kneeling in stone chapels no matter the weather, had made me appreciate the way a good chill could focus the mind.

Jovi might very well have been the most exciting thing that had ever happened to me.

But I knew what else he was, too.

I put the pieces together now, one after the next, like a puzzle.

He was a weapon—and an elite one—but he belonged to someone else. And he was Italian, so I could guess what sort of *someone else* that was and what kind of organization they were a part of.

I also paid far more attention to the things my father said to the men he was parading me around in front of—because it's always good practice to know what the people who have power over you are concerned with—so I also knew my father was under the impression that he had the upper hand over *our unpleasant friends from the south*.

It didn't take a genius to put these things together and come up with the implacable presence of a man made of stone in my bedroom.

Not to mention, I knew my father well enough to suspect that, as usual, he believed that he was the smartest man around.

Based on nothing more than his belief that he ought to have been.

I sat there with all these facts and puzzle pieces spinning around and around inside me, and I could feel the urge to react emotionally. To let that churning in my stomach turn into something far more precarious and nauseous, and let that tip over into the sort of sob that might blow out the walls—

But I didn't.

I breathed myself calm again, which was pretty much my superpower. Growing up the way I did, controlling my own reactions was often the only thing I had to hold on to in any given bad situation.

As I got older, I recognized it for the armor it was, too.

I decided I could use a little of both, here in the middle of my very first kidnapping. The one that might very well turn into my very first—

Well. I didn't really want to think about that.

If this was all the life I had left, I wanted to focus on living it.

Right now that meant my breath. It meant keeping my hands from going to sleep. It meant moving just enough to keep my muscles happy. It meant letting the silent room soothe me.

And it did, though I suspected that wasn't the point of it. Some people spent their whole lives running away from the thoughts in their own heads, and for them, I'd bet sitting in an empty room with nothing but the quiet would drive them mad.

I could tell that this room had been built to contain noise and let nothing in from the outside. I decided that meant that it had been made to be some kind of a media room. Because I didn't want to think what other sorts of rooms people built like this, with no windows save that one in the bathroom, but I was pretty sure wouldn't have budged even if I'd had a sledgehammer.

I sat. I breathed. At first, I tried to recite the long prayers we'd been forced to memorize at the convent, because I knew exactly how long each one of them took. But I grew bored with that, because I kept getting distracted by the memory of kissing Jovi. By the whole of this night and all of those moments that should have been awful, but hadn't been.

I decided, then and there, that there was no point in asking myself what was wrong with me.

The answer was nothing.

All things considered, I thought that I was stunningly healthy in the middle of what could best be described as a deeply unhealthy situation, none of it of my own making.

And I was considering how best to congratulate myself on all that robust mental health when the door opened.

I wanted to say something flippant about the room itself. How the silence was so intense it seemed more like humidity, pressing in against every nook and cranny of my skin, until I was certain I could feel it like a touch.

But something in the way Jovi was frowning at me as he strode toward me, no longer wearing his suit coat, stopped me.

It was so forbidding.

It was also, I fear, *hot*.

It made everything in me...*hum* itself to life again, if I was honest.

I said nothing as he came and stood before me, not even when he seemed to take too long gazing down at me, as if he was memorizing my face. As if he needed to memorize it, because—

When he reached out his hands, I ordered myself not to flinch. I didn't.

But no flinching was necessary anyway, because all he did was unlock my wrists from those cuffs.

And just like out there in the garage, he stood there for a moment and massaged them, one and then the next. Making certain that all the blood came back and was moving properly.

I knew that in my books, they called it *aftercare*.

But I decided that discretion was the better part of valor, and opted not to tell him that.

Jovi studied my face. When he muttered something under his breath, some kind of curse, I wondered what he saw.

Yet something in me knew better than to ask.

He pulled me up to my feet and then he led me out of that room with that big, hard hand of his guiding the way. This time it was on the back of my neck, propelling me out into the house ahead of him and up those stairs to the next level.

When we got to the door that waited for us on the landing a flight up, he paused. It was gloomy in this stairway, with no windows and only a dim light up on the wall. I could hear him breathing, and something about that felt unbearably intimate. My eyes drifted shut, but opened again when he put his hand on the door that waited there.

I could feel him, big and glowering and so impossibly beautiful, so exquisitely *him*, behind me.

"Tomorrow," Jovi told me roughly. "I will kill you tomorrow."

Then he opened the door and led me into what

looked like a perfectly normal, happy little flat, lit up from all the light that was pouring in from outside.

It took me longer than it should have to understand that it was daylight.

And if he didn't know that it was already tomorrow, I wasn't going to tell him.

Especially not when he turned me back around to face him, so I could see that look of anguish and desire all over his face, and took me in his arms at last.

CHAPTER SEVEN

He was ruined.

Wrecked.

Jovi had no idea what was happening to him. What had been happening to him ever since Rux had looked up from her book, met his gaze, and held it.

The attraction was bad enough. His body had always been his to command—the only thing that was entirely and only his—until now. This feeling inside him, this unbearable need, made him feel like someone else, some stranger unbound by the vows that had ordered the whole of his life. He could not understand how anyone lived through feeling like this, why it didn't cut them to their knees.

He didn't understand what his body was doing. It was a wild ride, and on some level, he might have understood it if it was only his cock, but there was all the rest of it, too. That outrageous pain in his chest. The surprising fragility of his own ribs.

Worse still, he felt...hot. Everywhere.

When he'd left her in that room below, he'd climbed the stairs to the living part of this house and had wondered if he was coming down with some kind of fever. If he was actually ill.

Because otherwise, he could not account for this. For any part of this.

His body did not feel like *his* any longer. It seemed to obey that heat inside him instead, that consuming, outrageous heat that seeped into every part of him, making him edgy. Making him *hungry*.

He'd tried to shake himself out of whatever spell he was under. He'd tried to remind himself that he was a professional, that this was what he had been raised and trained to do and not some kind of twisted date, and that he had things to accomplish here.

Promises to keep to the man who had allowed him to live.

Promises that were all that differentiated him from an upstart or an enemy, in his family's eyes.

Jovi could not make sense of the voice in him—some odd, alien voice—that wanted to know why he was allowing this to continue. Why, when he was by far the most powerful person in Il Serpente if fear alone was the metric, did he continue to bend the knee to those he could end as easily as anyone else he'd been assigned to handle?

These were treacherous thoughts, he'd thought. Dangerous thoughts.

Because Don Antonio had spared Jovi's life, but he had taken that life and made it his. There was not one thing Jovi had, including the air he breathed, that his uncle had not given to him by virtue of letting him live.

How could he possibly question that? It was the

foundation on which the whole of Jovi's existence stood.

He'd moved around the flat, determined to force himself back to normal by performing the usual tasks he would typically handle at a time like this. There were always tracks to be covered, competing exit scenarios to be plotted out in case one or another fell through, not to mention the more unsavory details comprising cleanup, disposal, staging if necessary, and all the rest of the things that Jovi had always accepted without the faintest hint of emotion.

Yet tonight—this morning, he corrected himself when he'd realized the sun had already come up outside—none of it sat well with him.

He didn't sit well with him.

Too many things seemed to be chasing each other around and around inside his head. Scraps of memories he rarely allowed himself to look at and would have denied he still carried inside him.

His mother dancing in the hall of the old villa, back when it was filled with color and life. She'd spun as if she was made of light and laughter and her dress spun out with her, making her look magical.

His father had watched her, a look of sheer delight on his face, before he'd tumbled her down into his arms and kissed her, thoroughly.

Jovi hadn't thought about that moment nearly forever. He hadn't allowed himself to remember that they'd been *happy*.

When he thought about his parents—and he tried his best not to think of them at all, and when he did, only as the traitor and the casualties of the traitor's betrayal—he thought about the end. About what their deaths had made his life. About what his father's desire for escape or justice or whatever he'd told himself he was doing had truly cost.

What he'd had to do to prove himself to his uncle ever since.

And who he'd become.

He'd found himself standing there in the center of that open living area with the light pouring in, not still at all. Not practicing to be an ice sculpture, the way he normally did, and without effort. But today he'd found himself unable to keep his edginess at bay.

Because all he could think about was Rux.

The *taste* of her. How was he meant to do his duty when the taste of her haunted him the way it did?

In his head, he heard long-ago laughter. His sisters' high-pitched voices. He saw himself, just a little boy, walking in the gardens and then looking up—and in the memory, it seemed as if he'd looked up at least seven stories—to take his father's hand—

He had forgotten that *he* had been happy, too.

And that suggested that he was not anything like happy now.

She had broken something in him, he'd told himself, roughly. That was clear. Rux had somehow found a weak spot in him that he would have sworn did not, could not exist. All over the world, people spoke of him in hushed, fearful tones, and for good reason. Every single one of them would have sworn up and down that there was no way into him. That there was no weakness and no access.

That Giovanbattista D'Amato was an impermeable block of ice and stone, a nightmare made flesh.

He did not know what to do with the discovery that he was as mortal and fallible as anyone else. What was next? Would he lose his head completely? Would he challenge his uncle? Betray his family?

It was unthinkable. This was all *unthinkable*.

He had repeated that word again and again until he'd decided that the fury growing within him was just that. Temper. Outrage.

He told himself that was a good thing. He told himself he was *relieved*.

Jovi had never experienced temper before, but in this case, it was clearly warranted.

And that was why he'd stormed downstairs, determined that he would put an end to this. She might not be afraid of him, but she would be. He would see to it.

But then, instead, he'd seen *her*.

Her dark gray eyes had found his and something about that had made that sharp, impossible pain in his chest worsen. He'd walked toward her and with every step, he'd realized that what he wanted to call temper was something else.

Something hotter. Something far more molten and dangerous.

And the next thing he knew, he'd brought her upstairs, out of that room that was more properly a cell, and into this flat.

Then he'd really blown it all to shit and pulled her into his arms.

Jovi supposed that somewhere, deep inside, he had the notion that he could treat her like every other woman he'd ever had, summarily discarded, and never thought of again.

Surely he could do the same with Rux.

Even though she made his heart *pound*, each jarring thump another indication of how ruined he was. Kissing her had changed him—*melted* him in ways he did not wish to look at more closely—but he was certain he could fix that.

He had to fix it.

So he took her in his arms and got his mouth on her once more. And then everything seemed to burn even brighter.

Especially him.

Because this time, she melted into him without any chains to hold her back. This time, she wrapped her arms around his neck, something Jovi would normally never allow, but it was different when it was Rux.

For many reasons, but most crucially, because the way she held on to him allowed him to kiss her that much more deeply. And he found that there was very little he wouldn't do for a result like that.

He kissed her and kissed her, and the flames that roared through him nearly took over everything—but he had the presence of mind to remember that they stood near windows. And that he knew better.

With what small part of *him* remained, he picked her up again and this time she held on and crossed her legs around him so her ankles dug into the small of his back and her thighs gripped him too. And when he made a groaning sort of sound that, she pulled her head back to look at him.

"Jovi—" she began.

"Quiet," he muttered, and kissed her, but he didn't let himself linger.

He also didn't put her down. With one hand, he cupped her spectacular ass as he went to make sure the door was locked and bolted. Then he walked through the main room with all its windows and into the dark cave of the bedroom in the back.

"You really do have a thing against windows, don't you?" she said as the darkness of the bedroom swallowed them whole.

"I have a thing against snipers," he replied shortly.

And he supposed it was a reminder of what kind of people they were and what kind of lives they'd both led that all she did was nod.

Jovi didn't need any lights to know where he was going, or any time for his eyes to adjust. He simply walked forward, waited until his shins found the bed, and toppled them both straight down into the mattress.

He didn't land with all of his weight on her, but he gave her some of it and felt that melting sensation inside intensify when she made a little sighing sound, a softer echo of the noise he'd made before.

And it was possible—*probable*—that lying down with her like this was a mistake, he acknowledged, but he didn't give a shit.

They were on a bed together and she was beneath

him and he thought that if he didn't make her come at least three times, he might explode.

He told himself that there was truth in *that*, anyway. There was only honesty in a woman's orgasm and men like his cousins who joked about not letting their women finish, or suspecting that they were faking—

All you're doing is telling on yourselves, he had told them once, and had only shrugged at the chorus of invective and character assassination. *If all you do is disregard a woman's pleasure, you might as well use your hand.*

Another thing his cousins hadn't cared for, particularly Carlo.

But he didn't need to remember the women he'd been with, or care about them at all, to appreciate the radical, intimate knowledge a woman's orgasm allowed him.

And once he *knew*, he didn't have to *feel*.

Jovi stretched out beside Rux. He took her jaw in his hand and he kissed her even more deeply than before, making it long, lingering. Making it dirty and deep.

And when she was writhing there beside him, he let his other hand move down the length of her body.

He didn't stop kissing her, but he quickly became consumed with the shape of her. Oh, he'd paid attention to her before. He hadn't been able to keep himself from noticing every detail—but this was different.

This wasn't work.

He gathered her wrists in one of his hands and stretched them high over her head. He made a low noise of approval as her breasts jutted out, and settled in beside her to finally free them from those ridiculous cotton pajamas she wore. He could have finessed the buttons, but he didn't—choosing instead to yank them free, sending the buttons scattering.

And he felt her shiver each time a button popped. It felt like a gift.

Jovi couldn't recall the last time he'd received anything like a *gift*.

When he finally spread the panels of the pajama top open, he could see that one of his suspicions had been true. That flush that started on her cheeks moved all the way down her neck to redden her breasts as well.

Clearly he had to taste it.

He started at her temple and took his time tracing that blush of hers. Over the arch of her cheekbone, then the cheek below. He skirted her distracting mouth, finding his way to the column of her neck instead. She smelled like candy and she tasted sweeter still, and for the first time in his life, Jovi found himself combating what could only be a sugar high.

Or maybe he wasn't combating it, he thought as he moved lower, using the hand that wasn't wrapped around her wrist to cup one breast. He held it up so he could bend his head, and get a taste of it. He took his time, and liked it when she shifted beneath him, her head thrashing back and forth on the bed.

"Jovi... *Please...*"

"I like it when you beg," he told her, his mouth against her skin. And when he felt her tremble, he wondered. What would it take to make her come simply from this?

He let go of her wrists and moved so he could cup both of her breasts at once. Then he bent his head to suck the nipple nearest to him deep into his mouth, while at the same time, he pinched the other one.

For a moment, she went stiff, and still. Then in the next, she made a high-pitched, keening sort of sound, and dug her heels into the mattress, lifting herself up.

But he didn't take advantage of that. Not yet. He rolled one nipple with his tongue and the other with his fingers, lazily. Slowly.

He played with her, and when her breath got short and choppy, he let go, switching his mouth and hands.

Then he started all over again.

And to his delight, she squeezed her thighs together and she rocked herself, arching her back higher and higher into his mouth and into his hand. Her own hands dug deep into his hair, gripping him hard, and all of it was the same driving, melting wildfire.

Until, when he pinched her just hard enough and let his teeth scrape her other nipple, Rux exploded.

He held her as she bucked and shook. And while she was distracted, he sat her up, stripping her of that pajama top and tossing it aside. He did the same with the pajama bottoms, and discovered several things at once.

First, she was even more beautiful than he had imagined. Second, he was able to tell this at a glance, because she apparently slept commando.

And best of all, he could see how ready she was as she lay there in total abandon, pink glistening.

He took his time removing his own clothes, until he was in nothing save his boxer briefs.

When he stretched out beside her again, her eyes were fluttering, and she had her arms tossed up overhead.

"I've never..." she managed to pant out.

"Is that the first time you've come?" Jovi asked, fascinated by the way the thought of that made his cock even harder.

"Of course not," she said, on a breathy sort of laugh. She rubbed her hands over her face and then looked at him, hitting him with all that deep gray. "But it was the first time I wasn't alone."

Once again, he felt that fundamental, animal need to take her apart in any way he could. To watch her shiver and shake while she lost herself. To be the reason she gave up control of her body and surrendered herself entirely to him.

So this time, he moved to the headboard, leaned back against it, and then pulled her into his arms with her back flush to his front. He tipped her head back so she was resting against his chest and her mouth was tipped up in his direction.

Because he had designs on that mouth.

"Show me," he told her, his voice as dark as the windowless room all around them. Darker.

He felt her jolt. Her eyes went wide, but he could see the heat in them as they connected with his. He could feel it work into him, too.

"Show you?" Rux asked.

"Make yourself come," he told her, and didn't pretend it wasn't a flat-out order. "Now."

And he knew something else when she didn't get

flustered. When all she did was sigh a little bit and melt against him.

He knew something about both of them. Something he'd understood about himself for a long while, but then, he had never truly experimented with power dynamics like this before. He knew that the women he'd been with hadn't been faking, but that didn't mean that they liked this particular dynamic. They liked his power. They liked his danger. They liked the fact that they could brag that they'd had sex with Antonio's favorite weapon.

He had never begrudged any of that, because he didn't care about them.

But Rux was something completely different. He could feel the truth of it in the dreamy way she slid her hands down her body, as if this was the most peaceful moment she'd ever had in her life.

Under his command. Her body surrounded by his. Carrying out his order.

He knew a whole lot of things about the two of them, then. He could feel it everywhere. He could feel that pain in his chest shift into something else, something more like anticipation. He could feel that melting inside him, but it seemed to melt directly into her as she skimmed her hand over her belly, and found her way between her legs.

And then she tipped her head back, closed her eyes, and began to rock her hips against her own fingers.

As Rux worked, he brushed her hair back and put his mouth on her shoulder, her neck. He reached down and made her shiver with his hands on her breasts, then licked his way across the goose bumps that created.

He pressed his thick, hard cock into the small of her back so she could feel how hungry he was for her.

When she started to get faster, clumsier, and her breath too jagged, he found his way to her mouth and licked his way inside once more.

So that this time, when she began to shudder and move and moan, he swallowed it all down.

All that truth and temptation.

All she had to give.

She was sobbing a little as she rode it out. Even when it was only aftershocks, he wanted to taste that, too, like it would make this odd, bone-deep recognition he felt when it came to her dissipate.

Or that was what he told himself he wanted, anyway.

He turned her over, so she was face down on the bed, all flushed cheeks and her skin faintly damp from all the work she'd done.

"What a good girl you are," he told her, his voice dark and approving. "So obedient."

"They said that obedient women will never rule the world," she told him, but she didn't open her eyes. She did smile, however. "But I don't think the people who say that have any idea how good obeying you can feel."

Something deep inside Jovi hitched, then shuddered at that. As if, somehow, she'd managed to reach a part of him, a piece of him, he wasn't sure he could identify himself.

He did not want to look at that too closely when he wasn't sure he could tolerate *feeling* it, so he made it about sex instead. He made it about understanding her in the only way he could, which was by exploring every square centimeter of that lush body of hers.

He started on her back side, and he took his time. There was the exquisite perfection of her shoulder blades. There was a deeply fascinating freckle in the small of her back. Her ass was beautifully rounded and heart-shaped from behind, and he already knew how he would fit his hands around her nipped-in waist and slam himself deep inside her. He could already feel how good it would be. It already felt like fate.

But not yet.

Jovi explored the tender underside of each of her ass cheeks, grazing both that dark furrow behind and the low pout of the softest, sweetest part of her. But he didn't pause there, no matter how it made her moan.

He kept going, down one leg all the way to her toes and then up again to do the same thing on her other leg.

Only to turn her over and start the whole thing over again on the front side of her marvelous body.

This time, he found every sweet little bit of magic she possessed. Narrow shoulders but heavy breasts, that slender waist that only made the flare of her hips more dramatic. Her thighs had gripped him tight and sure, and he liked that. She wasn't frail. She wasn't breakable.

That was a good thing, given the great many things he intended to do to her.

But first, there was this.

One last exercise of his control, one last lesson for her to learn about surrender.

Before they slept, anyway. He moved all over her, up and down and anywhere else that took his fancy, avoiding that plush, soft place between her legs.

And only when she was pressing her palms into her eyes, half laughing and half sobbing as she begged him and pleaded with him and made him growl in response, did he finally move to settle himself between her legs.

He pushed her thighs apart so he could drape her legs over his shoulders. He settled in, grabbing that round ass of hers in his hands, before he let himself go.

And then Jovi ate her alive.

And even when she came, screaming out his name and making all of that melting heat and terrible beating of his heart seem to burn too bright, Jovi kept his cock to himself. He told himself that he had all of this—her and, more concerning, *himself*—completely under control.

Completely and totally under his fucking control, even if it killed him.

CHAPTER EIGHT

I SLEPT HARD.

Maybe I passed out.

To be honest, I didn't really care either way. I toppled into a deep unconsciousness and as far as I could tell, I didn't move at all.

When I woke up, I was disoriented. I felt heavy in a number of marvelous ways, but I was in that dark bedroom that clearly wasn't my own. There was no light. It took a good couple of breaths for everything to come flooding back to me.

And when it did, it was red-hot.

The important part was that I was still alive. And yet, as embarrassing as it probably ought to have been for me to admit even to myself, I had lived my best life right here in this bed.

I snuggled deeper into the bed, realizing two things in rapid succession. First, that Jovi wasn't here in this bedroom with me. Maybe that wasn't a surprise.

What was, however, was that he had clearly let me sleep.

Just...*let me sleep.*

This did not strike me as typical kidnapper behavior.

Then again, neither did what had happened between us before I'd fallen asleep.

Further investigation revealed even more fascinating discoveries. My hands weren't tied. Neither were my feet. When I glanced over at the door, I could see a ring of light around the frame where it was shut tight, though I didn't know if that was daylight or electricity.

I could have slept for fifteen minutes or ten years. I couldn't tell.

It was possible—really, it was *likely*—that he'd locked me in here. But I couldn't bring myself to worry about that too much. It was still a major upgrade from a chair in a bare room with my hands tied above my head.

Though if I was honest, that hadn't been too bad, either.

Or maybe you're used to so many terrible things that you think slightly less *terrible things are a delight*, a voice that sounded a lot like Katarzyna countered inside my head.

Though if it was really my stepmother, she was far more likely to toss back a hefty pour of her preferred *wodka* and intone something like, *No one ever promised that things would be good, so if you simply decide that it is—no matter how revolting—it is the same thing in the end.*

I found myself smiling, as if she was really here and had really said such a thing in her typically dour way.

I do not lift spirits, Ruxandra, she had told me once. *I drink them.*

I was shocked to discover that I was going to miss her, when I had never thought much about my other stepmothers. Then again, none of *them* had been so close to my age.

I turned on my side and let everything that had happened since Jovi had appeared before me like the hottest possible apparition flow through me. I was very tempted to lie where I was and daydream my way back through all of the things he'd done to me last night. Or earlier this morning, as the case may be.

Again and again, since even the faintest touch of memory made me feel warm all over.

Though what was infinitely more tempting than that was the idea that Jovi himself was right there on the other side of the door.

Because all I really wanted to do was touch him again.

I decided to forgive myself both retroactively and in advance for any foolish things I did while under the influence of that man.

"I'm just a girl," I whispered to myself, beneath my breath. But I smiled into the dark. "I can only be expected to do so much."

I sat up and swung my legs over the side of the bed, taking stock of my body. This body that had been entirely and only mine for my whole life until last night.

He had taken me bodily from my father's fortress of a house. Then he had taken things I hadn't known I'd been saving only for him. That I was *pleased* I'd never shared with anyone else—because even though I'd been kept locked away my whole life, there were always moments that could bloom into bigger things. I knew a lot of the girls in the convent who had "prayed together."

And there were always the guards with greedy looks and too-long glances, more than happy to take a bite of the forbidden fruit.

But I'd never indulged.

Now I thought I knew why.

Now, I thought, he'd made my body his as if it had been destined for him all along.

I knew my body all too well. I despaired over the flaws I saw in it that I liked to pick apart in the mirror. I admired its strength. What I really liked was the way the most dangerous man I've ever met looked at this body. How he'd moved his hands over me in seeming awe and wonder. How he'd used his mouth like some kind of benediction.

After all those days and nights in lonely rooms in both the convent and my father's house, it seemed to me that I had finally found holy ground.

By this point, I realized that I could see in the dark well enough, so there seemed little reason to linger where I was when he was the only thing on my mind. I could see my pajamas crumpled in a heap on the floor, so I pulled on the little shorts and only remembered that he'd torn all the buttons off the top when I shrugged it on.

The girl I'd been before him paused, because *she* had never let another person see her naked since she'd been a baby.

But the woman I was now decided I didn't really care if the man who'd had his hands and mouth all over my body saw that body in the light.

Though even as I thought that, the idea made me shiver a little all the same.

Because the darkness was one thing. There were places to hide. Or maybe I just wanted to believe that there were.

I swallowed, but I moved over to the door anyway.

I put my hand on the doorknob and accepted that this was a moment of truth, in its way. Had he locked me in here? Was this just another cell?

He was my captor. He was my only lover.

But which one was he right now?

I held my breath and tried the knob—

And when it turned easily in my hand, I pulled the door open.

I felt emotion pummel me then, as something alarmingly close to a sob threatened to erupt from deep inside me.

Maybe because I couldn't remember the last time I hadn't been locked away. In the convent. In my bare little room in the dormitories there. In my father's house, sequestered on my own lonely hall, guards at the end to keep me there. And sometimes, depending on my father's mood, with the bolt thrown on my bedroom door—to which only he had the key.

I had no idea what expression could possibly be on my face as I let all the light that greeted me wash over me, but I didn't fight it. I didn't stop, either. I let all that shocking emotion roll through me as it would, then I let it go.

And it was only when I was sure I wasn't about to break down in sobs that I looked around and found

Jovi watching me with a curious look on his face from where he sat at the counter in the open plan kitchen, a tablet in his hand.

"Good morning," I said, with laughable courtesy, given the circumstances.

But he didn't laugh, of course.

"It is afternoon," he told me, expressionless. But with a hint of reprimand in his tone, as if I'd been lazing about like some kind of spoiled princess after a night out partying.

For some reason, that made *me* laugh.

"Yes," I said, nodding. "It's very important to keep the correct time in a circumstance like this. And I do apologize. I usually prefer to wake up bright and early to fully experience the breadth and depth of traumatic kidnaps. My bad."

Jovi did not respond to that. He only watched me, darkly.

This was fine with me because there were important details to consider, I realized belatedly. Such as the fact that he was wearing a pair of what looked like athletic trousers. They were black, sat low on his hips, and, more importantly, they were the only thing he was wearing.

Meaning I could see the full glory of his chest.

I had felt it last night. I'd driven myself happily mad against it, and even now my hands longed to do a better job with it. I wanted to find my way over every ridge and scar. I wanted to commit them all to memory.

I wanted to brand him on the inside of me, so he would always be mine.

What I noticed most of all was the tattoo over his heart. It was a circle of words in all-black ink, stamped deep into his skin. With a snake coiled in the middle of it.

"You should eat," Jovi said in a gruff voice.

His eyes were still dark, but I imagined that I could read them better now. There was that intensity that I assumed was simply *him*. But there was more now. Something else that I very much wanted to call...*care*, maybe? *Affection* seemed like an overreach. And yet.

"Must I?" I asked, because I didn't feel like I had anything even faintly resembling an appetite—

Yet the moment I thought that, I was suddenly aware that my stomach felt hollow. That I wasn't simply hungry, I was *famished*.

"You must," he said shortly.

He switched off his tablet and set it down. He turned, and as I watched with a sort of astonishment that made every beat of my heart feel jarring and strange, he began to pull food out of the refrigerator. Not food, *ingredients*.

And then, with only a fulminating glance in my direction, he proceeded to prepare me a meal.

Eggs with vegetables and meat. A bit of a salad. Fruit.

When he was finished, he slid the plate across the counter, and pointed at the seat in front of it that he wished me to take.

I was still standing there at the door to the bedroom in my half-opened pajama top, staring at this man I knew to be perhaps the scariest on earth.

Who had just prepared me a cheerful-looking brunch, from scratch.

"What if I don't like eggs?" I asked, and I didn't even know where the question came from, because I liked eggs just fine.

In any case, he only lifted a brow. "I did not ask what you liked. I told you to eat. I cannot have you fainting away, Rux."

"Is this like fattening up the calf for slaughter?"

But even as I asked that, my stomach was grumbling. I moved over to the counter, took the seat he indicated I should, and tried my level best not to fall upon the meal he'd made me like a wild animal.

"I will almost certainly kill you tomorrow," he said, almost offhandedly. The way he had once already. "But in the meantime, *baggiana*, I have a lot of extremely physical demands I intend to make of you. You will need to keep up your strength."

I froze, my fork halfway to my mouth. "What do you mean by *extremely physical demands*?"

I cautioned myself that he could mean something unpleasant. But my entire body was certain he meant something deeply pleasant indeed.

He jutted his chin toward my plate. "Eat, Rux. Now."

So I did the only thing I could in a situation like this.

I ate.

When I was done, I went to wash my plate but he took it from me. He waved me away, and even though I suspected that he would have preferred it if I stood there quietly and waited for his next command, I couldn't do it.

"Why do you know how to cook?" I asked.

He wasn't looking at me, and still I could see affront all over his body. Along with scars and smooth muscle on his sculpted back. "What kind of question is this? I am Sicilian."

"I was under the impression that most Italian men—"

"I am Sicilian," he corrected me, with an edge in his voice. But when he turned to face me, I could see that his eyes were gleaming in that way that I was pretty sure was his version of laughter. "I am only Italian second, and under duress, you understand."

"I thought most men from your region had a collection of grandmothers to do all the cooking for them. Or mothers, in a pinch."

"There are always women to cook meals," he said, but there was something about the way he said it that made me frown at him. He shrugged. "My mother died a long time ago and my grandmother only cooks sometimes, these days. There are many other women in my family, and it is true that they can also do these things, and they do. But I am not always in Sicily. And when I am not, I prefer to cook for myself."

I considered that. "Well. You're very good at it."

"Do you know how to cook?" he asked me.

I laughed. "Boris Ardelean's only child, no better than a kitchen drudge? Certainly not. My father believes that common domestic tasks are below him, and therefore, below me. Though, confusingly, he also believes that a woman's role is to be silent and decorative and obedient. Just as long as her hands are soft and she remains appropriately slender and docile at all times, he thinks this is the epitome of all that is classy."

Jovi studied me in the remains of my Christmas tree pajamas. "You do not?"

"I think," I said carefully, diplomatically, even though my father was not in the room and I wouldn't have been speaking like this if he was, "that anyone who is concerned with whether or not something is *classy* doesn't have much class to begin with. But we are talking about a man who would never cook for his own wife. He would see that as a direct assault upon his masculinity."

Though now, as I said a thing like that, I had a better grasp of the implications.

"Then he is not much of a man," Jovi said after a moment, and I could tell that we were both picturing the things he'd done with his wicked mouth between my legs, making me cry out so loud I was shocked the Policie České Republiky had not broken down the doors. "But this is not a surprise."

I could feel his tongue again as if he was still crouched there between my legs with his hands holding me high and open. I wanted more of that, even though I thought it might actually be the thing that killed me.

But I couldn't really believe he was *talking* to me. I wanted to keep it going. "But the men you work for are better?"

I could tell it was a mistake immediately. He went hard and cold in a blink. I'm not sure he moved. He simply…changed.

"Who is it that you think I work for?" he demanded, in that softly intimidating way of his.

I could feel my eyes go wide. "I have no idea." I pointed at the tattoo on his chest. "Somebody, though. I'm betting."

He put a hand on his heart as if he'd forgotten the tattoo was there. Then he looked down, as if he'd forgotten his heart was there, too.

When he looked up again, he looked almost... shaken. Alarmed. Something like that.

He did not have to tell me that this was not a normal reaction for him. That he did not usually feel these things.

Or anything.

"This is not a conversation we need to have," he said with that quiet command. That I had responded to before he touched me, but now...

I could feel it. Licks of sweet, wild fire, everywhere.

"You said you were a man of vows," I reminded him. "What does that mean? Is that what your tattoo says?"

We were still standing in the flat's sprawling galley kitchen that was outfitted with sleek, impressive appliances, none of them offering the slightest personal hint about the man who seemed so comfortable here that he had fresh groceries in the refrigerator. Nothing in the flat was personal, I realized then. This was a way station, not a home.

I was glad the kitchen opened up to the living area, because Jovi didn't need any help taking up all the air there was.

And I needed to pay more attention to my breath.

Meaning, I needed to stop holding it.

"You should be very careful asking questions, *baggiana*," he warned me. "I am not certain you want the answers."

"I thought I made this clear," I said at once. "I want everything."

"This I doubt."

"You're the only one who knows how much life I have left to live," I reminded him, and the funniest thing was that I felt almost…comfortable that I was so fully in his hands. Life, death, and all the pleasure in between. It didn't feel like a risk, it felt *right*. "What I want is every last thing I can find in that period of time. That's all." I blew out a breath. "And only you can give it to me, Jovi. Only you."

He moved toward me then, and I had the sensation it wasn't of his own volition. There was that wondering sort of look on his face once more as he fit his hand to my jaw.

I watched his eyes flare when I nestled my cheek more deeply into his grip.

"My family operates on loyalty," he told me after a moment, his voice a dark, thrilling scrape of sound. "My father chose disloyalty and paid for it. So it has never been enough for me to express my own loyalty or honor. I've had to prove it. Live it." His dark eyes scanned mine. "Become it."

"What did your father do?" I dared to ask.

He looked almost shocked. And I had a little bolt of intuition then. I would have sworn on anything and everything I was that he had never talked about these things before with any other woman.

Or anyone else, for that matter.

"My family runs a very particular kind of family business," he said. Eventually.

Neither one of us named that business. Neither one of us chose any one of the many words and phrases we could have used to describe the kind of business I was certain he was part of. It was unnecessary. I had always referred to my own father as *an entrepreneur* for the same reasons.

"My father did not wish to be part of this business," Jovi continued, with a faint note of surprise in his voice, as if he could not believe he was talking about such things. "He became embittered by it. He wanted out, not only for himself, but for the whole of his family. That might have been allowed, since he was the brother of the family's head, but he wanted to take the business apart as well."

I wanted to hold him. I settled for putting my hand over his, there where it rested against my face.

Jovi frowned as if this story caused him pain, or maybe my touch did, but he kept going. Stiffly. "He began talking to the people who could do the dismantling. It was discovered. Consequences followed swiftly."

I thought about *consequences*. About the kind of consequences that were typically rendered in a world like ours. He didn't have to tell me what had happened to his family in any detail. I could guess.

And I thought, too, about the ways loyalty was demanded but even more so, how it was cultivated. If the only person in your life who could help you or harm you was a tyrant, well. I supposed that some people might have *standards*. They might hold themselves to some higher level of morality, because they could. But it was my experience that when the kinds of people Jovi and I knew took charge of a child and set themselves up as a cruel god who had the power of life and death over them…

There were all kinds of consequences when you lived the kinds of lives we had.

Something in me shuddered, near enough to another sob, when I thought about all the ways that Jovi and I were the same.

I didn't say this out loud. I wasn't that far gone.

So I did what I could. I went up on my toes and while he looked at me with something like wariness, I slid my hands onto his hard jaw, and cupped his face.

But that wasn't enough, so I leaned in. And I kissed him.

Not the devouring, life-altering kissing that we'd been doing. Not that wild burn that consumed everything, leaving nothing in its wake but ash and longing.

I could feel that fire inside me, and I could taste it on his lips, but this kiss wasn't about that.

This kiss was comfort, understanding. This kiss was compassion and empathy.

This kiss was all these strange and overwhelming things I felt for him that didn't feel any less real for being so fast, so sudden.

Truth be told, I had never felt anything more real in my life.

I kissed him like he was a wish granted, like I was sealing the deal on something magic, some marvel that was only ours.

The kiss shook through me. I could feel it in him, too.

When he pulled away, I gazed up at him and found the world was gone. Everything had narrowed down to this. The two of us, eye to eye. The sound of our breath and the way we seemed fused together, into one.

My hands on his face while his hands had come to grip my upper arms.

And I knew something without reservation or shame, without argument or concern. We *belonged*, Jovi and me.

We were made for this, this dark communion. No matter what happened. No matter what he did because of vows he'd made to monstrous men. I would forgive him.

I already had.

And I think he saw that on my face, because he made a low, helpless sort of growl and then he was swinging me up in his arms. He carried me back into the bedroom, laid me out on the bed, and taught me that the things I'd only read about in books were far, far better on this side of the page.

He let me explore him. I traced the muscles on his back, the strength of his biceps, and the planes of his chest. I became obsessed with his male nipples that I found I could lick and tease as he'd done to me. I moved from one to the next, the way he'd showed me, and paused to make sure I licked my way along every letter that circled his heart, and the snake slapped over it.

"*Chiù nniuri ri mezzannotte nun pò fari,*" he muttered at me, as if it was some kind of prayer. Then he translated himself. "It can't get any darker than midnight, surely."

As if I was torturing him. I flushed with pleasure.

I followed the hair on his chest, glorying in the way it thickened as I moved down south, and when I got to that intriguing V that seemed to point the way to exactly where I most wanted to go, I thought he would stop.

But he didn't.

Instead, he moved me so that he was sitting on the edge of the bed and I was kneeling before him, deliciously caged between his legs.

"I've never done this before," I whispered, my hands trembling as I held myself up with my palms on his thighs.

Something dark and fierce moved over his face then, and took root.

"You remember what I did to you last night," he said.

It wasn't a question. It was a demand, I realized. He wanted me to remember exactly what he had done. In detail. And so I did.

And as I did, I could feel myself ripen. I could feel that soft heat take me over as if he was licking into me all over again.

"It's the same idea," he told me. "Less a dish of ice cream, more a cone."

I set myself to the task happily. I slid my hands up, reached into his boxer briefs, and pulled all of him out.

And he was beautiful. He made my mouth water. Everything about him was thick and long, hard and big.

So astonishingly big that I was intimidated.

But I thought about ice cream cones, and how a person didn't go shoving the whole thing in her mouth at once.

So I started the way I would approach a cone. As if I was at a seaside, where I always imagined the best ice cream cones would be sampled, not that I'd ever seen the sea.

I licked my way over the tip first, humming a little as I went because he tasted so good.

He tasted like heat and our own wildfire. He tasted exactly as a man should, and though I had nothing to compare it to, I was confident no man alive could possibly taste better than he did. Just as no man was as beautiful.

I was enjoying myself, but the more attuned I became to his responses, the better I got. When I sucked him into my mouth, he groaned. When I wrapped my hands around the base of his shaft and took him as deep as I could into my mouth, he began muttering a string of filthy Sicilian curse words that I did not require translation to understand.

He let me play and experiment and what I got in return were the sounds he made, the way he dug his fists into my hair, and that molten heat between my own legs that had me squirming where I knelt.

And then, at a certain point, everything shifted. He

sat up straighter and took his hands out of my hair so that he could grip the sides of my head instead, and that easily, that quickly, he changed everything.

He took control.

I could feel my whole body surrender to his mastery as he slid himself in and out of my mouth, using me as he would, making me soar.

I could feel a trembling start deep down inside me, and it almost felt like grief, because I wanted so badly to concentrate on him. To make this all about him, the way it had been all about me before.

But there was no helping it. It was out of my control, like everything else.

And this was what sent me skyrocketing over the edge.

I squeezed my thighs together and began to rock myself and his thrusts were a little bit harder. He went a little bit deeper.

And then, as I broke into pieces, I tasted the flood of him on my tongue—a deep salt heat.

I drank down every drop. I shattered while I did it.

And for a long time, we stayed like that. Me, spent, still on my knees with my face on his thigh. Jovi sat on the bed, propping himself up with one hand, as he played with my hair, my cheek. As he murmured things I wasn't sure he even knew he was saying.

"We cannot stay in Prague," he told me after some while, his voice gritty.

My eyes were closed and I was still trying to catch my breath, but the import of his words hit me. Hard.

If *we* were leaving Prague, that meant he didn't intend to kill me in this house.

It meant that things had changed.

But I knew better than to crow about that. Or even to question him. Maybe I was afraid that if I did, he'd change his mind.

Instead, I turned my head slightly and pressed a kiss to his thigh. "All right."

His voice, if anything, was grittier when he replied. "It has not yet been twenty-four hours. Once we passed that marker, likelihood of getting caught in a snare increases."

All my limbs felt weighted down, but I managed to shift my hand and I traced patterns on his heavy quad muscle, currently acting as my pillow while I knelt there. His fingers moved through my hair, smoothing out the inky-black strands as if he found them precious. It would have been unbearable enough to make me cry if I could have processed it then, but I couldn't. I didn't.

I could only drift in the sweetness of this. I could only live in it.

"Where will we go?" I asked.

"Sicily."

I looked at him, confused. "Isn't that the last place you should go? With me?"

His mouth tightened. "It is the last place they will think to look for me. Until they hear that the assignment is complete, they will assume I am doing what is necessary somewhere else. It will buy some time."

Time, I decided, sounded lovely. It sounded the way I felt, gazing at him with his fingers in my hair.

Maybe, with time, I'd figure out if it was even possible to process...all of this.

"It is better if I appear to be traveling alone." He sounded fully grim then. "Do you understand what I mean?"

I thought I might, but I wanted him to tell me. So all I did was shake my head, there where he could feel it.

He tipped my head back so I was looking at him, and it was as if all the constellations in the sky somewhere above us changed position and found a new firmament there in his gaze.

I held my breath.

"I will need you to stay out of sight and quiet for some time. There is only one way to achieve this, practically speaking. I will knock you out and keep you out, then transport you out of Czechia."

"You do love to give a girl choices," I whispered. "I've never heard of such a thing as a woke weapon before."

His head tilted slightly to one side. But his eyes were gleaming. He was laughing. I knew he was.

"This is not a matter of offering choices. I am telling you what must occur."

He sounded as forbidding as ever, but the thing was... I knew better. Everything was changed. *He isn't going to kill me.* And there was a gap between not being killed and living happily ever after, I knew that. I did.

Although, given who we were, maybe not quite so big of a gap after all.

But in any case, I wanted to make him mine, and I wanted to be a part of the *we* who left Prague together. I wanted to make all of this my own, and not just because that was the easiest way to make a bad thing good.

Because I didn't think it was bad. I didn't think it was terrible.

I wanted more.

"You can do what you want with me," I told him. I tilted my head a bit to show him my neck, where long ago—it felt like a lifetime ago when it was only last night—he had traced his fingers down the side of my neck and talked to me of *blood chokes*. "All I ask is that you make it good."

For a moment, he looked stunned. In the next, I actually saw a flash of his teeth, as before my very eyes, Giovanbattista D'Amato, Il Serpente's deadliest weapon, smiled.

It almost made me come again, just at the sight. It hit me like a bolt of sensation, directly between my legs.

"As you wish," Jovi told me.

And then he hauled me up from my knees and dragged me over him to straddle his lap. He gripped my head, palming the back of it, and kissed me, dirty and deep.

As he did, he reached between us and speared his fingers into all of my molten heat, and he was deliciously, deliberately ungentle. As if he knew my hunger had teeth.

When he found the heart of me, he pressed his thumb there as he slid a finger inside my body.

Then, for a long, heated while, there was only his thumb, his finger, and his mouth on mine, demanding and marvelous.

He added a second finger, and I sighed a little bit against him as he stretched me, but I took it.

With his other hand, he gripped my neck. And kept right on kissing me, deep and carnal.

There was a pressure between my legs, a pressure plus a glorious heat and longing.

There was also a pressure on my neck, and that grip became a little bit harder and then a little bit harder still. And the more I bucked against it, the more my hips moved and the more I delivered myself into his hands.

I began to shiver, and he growled in approval.

"Come, Rux," he ordered me. "Come hard on my hand and deliver yourself to me."

And I did it. I obeyed him.

I clenched down hard on his fingers and sensation ripped through me, so intense it was almost like it hurt—

But the hurt was good. It was so good.

And his hand was on my throat, tighter and tighter, and just as the storm in me exploded I felt him press even harder.

Everything was delicious, bright hot and delirious.

Then it went dark.

And when I woke up, I was in Sicily.

CHAPTER NINE

I WAS GROGGY. My eyes were heavy, and it felt like there was sand in my throat.

My throat, I thought, and that penetrated the strange fog I was in.

I lifted my hand for my throat, expecting it to feel swollen and strange, but it felt the same as it always had. The fog receded a bit. I felt myself come back as if I'd been somewhere far, far away, and I understood.

It was me who was different.

I sat up then and found myself tangled in the sheets of a simple bed that was the only piece of furniture in an otherwise bare room. But it wasn't just any room. The walls were paneled, the ceiling frescoed, and the floor gleamed with age and wealth. I found myself pulling the sheet around me as I got to my feet, making my way gingerly and carefully over to the huge, floor-to-ceiling windows that I realized when I drew closer were doors.

Outside, I saw a ruined garden gleaming in the soft light. I saw lush trees in every direction. A mountain covered in scrub pine, rocks, and wildflowers set into deep, brown earth.

I opened the doors and stepped out onto the balcony and found the air sultry, like an embrace. And when I turned my head, I could see the sea.

Not only the sea. There was a city lying there between more hills, but it was the sea that caught at me. I'd never seen it before, that waiting, wondrous blue. I couldn't believe that I was near to it now. That I was surrounded by water instead of locked into the land.

I swore I could feel the difference inside me, as if I'd always been meant to find my way to a place by the sea.

I could not hear another human, but that didn't make it quiet. There was a riot of birds, wheeling and soaring all around. There was the rustle of wind through the trees and bushes, all of it scented of salt and lemon.

I left the tall windows open to let it all in and turned back to the bedroom that felt elegant in its complete simplicity, realizing that I didn't actually know if Jovi had dressed me at all. And it turned out I had more feelings—sensations—about the notion of being transported naked, though I wasn't sure why that made a difference when it was still him doing it.

I lifted my hand and smelled my own skin, certain that he'd washed me. I didn't smell like any of the products I used at home. I also didn't smell like him.

Turned out, that made a whole set of new feelings swirl around inside me.

Down at the foot of the bed, I found a set of loose, flowing trousers and a simple T-shirt. I pulled them on, though I wondered about them, too. Where had he gotten them? Had he gone shopping after he'd knocked me out in Prague? Did he carry women's clothing with him wherever he went?

But something in me knew he did not. The provenance of these clothes might be questionable, but I knew—the way I knew the shape of my own body and the taste of his kiss—that I was the only woman he'd ever thought to dress.

There was nothing like a mirror in this gracefully minimal room, so I smoothed my hands over my hair and had the same moment of trepidation I always did when I beheld a closed door. I held my breath as I turned the knob. And let it out again when the door opened with a faint squeak, as if to remind me that this was not a grotesque new build like my father's fortress.

That this was a house steeped in its own grandeur.

I made my way through the hushed, beautiful place, expecting to turn some corner or go down the stair and find the actual living area—filled with cozy keepsakes or even a comfortable sofa or a rug—but I never did.

It was a beautiful house, rambling and magnificent. It was airy and architecturally stunning, with views of the distant sea from every window, and the city that sprawled between it and me. But it was only the *bones* of the place. As if the people who lived here once had moved out a long, long time ago, leaving only the odd antique cupboard and incidental, artistic chair behind.

Walking through these empty rooms didn't make me muse on minimalism and modern art in the form of everyday objects and spaces, it made me want to cry, as if the house itself *ached* for its own storied past.

Finally, I found my way to the ground floor and

toward more windows that overlooked the garden in the back of the house. I went toward it, opening up one of the grand doors and finding my way out onto a bisected stair that led down toward the untended, overgrown garden that still showed signs of intense planning sometime long in the past.

It was only when I was halfway down that I realized that Jovi was there.

He was sitting so still, in the shade of the largest tree, that I hadn't seen him. My gaze had slid right over him like he was a statue.

But once I saw him, it was as if that current of heat snapped back into place between us once more. I was electrified. And I could see that he was, too.

Another thing I knew like the blood in my veins, the breath in my lungs.

I realized once I hit the paving stones that my feet were bare, but I didn't mind. I crossed the small courtyard that was more acrobatic weeds than elegant stone, then moved my way through the overgrown grass to Jovi's chair.

Once there, I obeyed the whisper of something like intuition deep inside me, and went to my knees before him.

And it was like something between us...erupted.

The look on his face was not cold. It was not at all remote. The intensity I saw there was almost overwhelming, but I didn't look away.

And the strangest part of it was, I did not feel the least bit submissive. I felt powerful. I felt *whole*.

More than that, when Jovi looked at me, I felt entirely seen.

"You are a beautiful terror," he told me, his voice a low sort of scrape that made my skin seem to tingle in its wake. "What am I to do with you, Rux?"

His hand was on my cheek, and I leaned into it, letting out a sigh as he traced the plumpness of my lower lip and the curve it made.

"Whatever you like," I said, and I meant it. But I also liked the way it made his eyes go dark and hot. "I thought I made that clear."

I watched him swallow and it wasn't lost on me that the fact he was showing me his reactions was monumental. He was showing me *everything*. He had melted away all the ice and peeled back the stone and what I was seeing was *him*.

I accepted that as the gift that I knew it was.

Because even if I'd managed to convince myself that a man as widely and rightly feared as Giovanbattista D'Amato had a vast circle of friends and endless intimates to choose from, seeing this house of his was like seeing the deep, unhealed wound inside him.

A beautiful house of empty rooms instead of a home.

He pulled me forward and I lifted my chin as I knelt up taller. Then he took his time examining me. As if looking for signs that something had happened to me, somewhere between Prague and here.

"How long did we travel?" I asked. I did not ask about the details. I thought maybe the bit of fog was a blessing.

"The travel itself was not long. There were certain

protocols necessary to leave Czechia without causing comment. But this was easily enough achieved."

I considered asking him how he'd transported me here. But since I suspected it was in a manner that wouldn't require a passport even if he'd had mine in hand, I chose not to.

Having an imagination was not always helpful, and I wasn't sure I wanted to put mine to work on this. Not when what mattered was the fact that I was here, now. That I was out of Prague. That my father had no idea where I was and no control over what I might do next.

When Jovi was done with his extremely thorough examination, he lifted me from the ground and settled me on his lap, my back to his chest. And once again, I had the strangest sensation that I was whole. That this was home. That *he* was.

I didn't tell him that, either. I held it as close to me as he was holding me.

I breathed out and let myself…melt into him.

He held me there as the birds called to each other up above us and the sun fell into patterns of light through the tree's leaves. I could feel his heart beating, as if it was a part of me. I could feel mine doing its best to match his rhythm.

For a few moments it felt as if we were one. The very same person.

My trousers floated over his hard thighs, tugged back and forth by that sea breeze. I could feel his cock against my back, nestled in tight between us. I could feel the heat we made and the warmth of the sun. I could smell the rich, deep green of the tangled garden behind us.

I had never felt like this before. I searched for the right word and when I found it, my heart seemed to stutter.

Content.

Even though, something in me understood that *contentment* was a mirage. This was Sicily. The men who wanted me dead as a lesson to my father lived here. There was nothing about my presence here that wasn't poised on the edge of a knife.

I blew out a shaky breath. "This is a beautiful house." I tried to focus on the sprawling old building that rose up before us and preened in the light without a care for how its cracks showed. Or how the creeping vines that had spread all over one of its walls looked like they might actually tear it down. On the one hand, I thought these details made it even more magnificent.

But then I thought about all those rooms I'd wandered through, filled with only light. "Though it looks…lonely, don't you think?"

I could feel his body tense, if only slightly, below mine.

"This is nothing more than a graveyard," he replied, shortly. But he didn't put me off him. He didn't let go. If anything, I thought he held me a little bit tighter.

I wished that I could see his face when he'd said that. *A graveyard.* I wondered if he meant that literally, and I was happy that he couldn't see my expression as I doubted that I was keeping it under control.

But I was certain that if I asked him too many questions, he would tell me even less.

I bit my tongue, and I felt him shift—slightly—beneath me. "After the consequences for my family were carried out, I went to live in my uncle's house."

He said that with no inflection. As if the consequences that were carried out were practical and acceptable. But if that was the case, there would have been no need for him to live with someone else. It didn't take any particular, deep insight to understand that what had happened here had been terrible. Brutal.

I suspected that when he said this was a graveyard, he meant it. But I still didn't speak.

"This house stood unattended for a long time," Jovi told me, quietly. Almost as if he was talking aloud to himself. "No one would dare loot it, given its connection to my uncle, but it became kind of ghost story in its own right. *Come to the villa, see if you can spend the night*, that sort of thing."

"There are ghosts here," I said softly. "That's clear."

"There are ghosts," he agreed, and he sounded... not exactly *happy* about that. Resigned, maybe. "And I know all their names."

"Jovi..." I whispered.

"They came in the night," he said, his voice a low ribbon of sound, almost a ghost itself. "They wanted it to be terrifying, like a nightmare, and it was." I could feel some kind of tremor go through him. "You know how these things go. There are prices for betrayal. My parents paid. My sisters paid." I could have sworn I heard a catch in his voice then, but I couldn't look back to see any evidence of it on his face. "I paid in a different way."

"Are you still paying?" I whispered.

"I will pay until the day I die," he told me, in that same resigned voice he used before.

It broke my heart.

But he still didn't let me turn around. He held me against him and even put his chin on the top of my head. And I felt certain that I was not the only one basking in what felt like the only bit of tenderness I'd ever known. Something almost healing.

As long as I didn't look him the eye, I thought that maybe it could last forever. Maybe this beautiful day would turn into always, like dreams always seemed to do.

I didn't pinch myself, because I didn't have to. I knew it was real.

I also knew better than to believe in *always*.

"The first two years at my uncle's house were an adjustment," Jovi continued after a while. "But adjusting was what was required of me, so I did it. And when I came of age, he gave me this house and all its contents. Everything my family had left behind. I sold it all off, as fast as I could."

"Wasn't it already yours?" I asked.

I could tell it was the wrong question. "That was a matter of debate," he said.

And I could imagine how that went. This was a lovely house. It was likely worth a lot of money, too. I could see the sort of family Jovi had arguing over who got to profit from all those consequences. I could also understand—having met so many men like him—why a man like Jovi's uncle would hold on to it. Better to use a tool as a weapon if your goal was to cause pain.

It seemed to have worked beautifully.

"Why did you sell everything?" I dared ask.

"I do not mind the ghosts," Jovi told me darkly. "It's the memories I can't abide."

I felt restless, or maybe—really—I was agitated on his behalf. I shifted myself around on his lap so I could look at him.

"What is your life here like?" I asked him. "What do you do in all your empty rooms? Wait for the garden to take you, too?"

He looked back at me, but he didn't quite manage to get his impassive mask back into place. "You ask a lot of questions for someone who was gamely going into a marriage that would have crushed her. Into dust."

I shook my head at him. "Not *gamely*," I corrected him. "Never *gamely*. I never once, in all of my dealings with my father, actually surrendered to him. I made nice. I bided my time. I accepted my unpleasant fate because there was nothing else to do. But that's not the same thing as *acquiescing*. Sooner or later, one of them—my father or whatever pig he married me off to—would underestimate me. Forget about me. And then I would be free." He was frowning back at me, so I leaned in a little closer. "I was only ever *biding my time*, Jovi. What have you been doing?"

He stood up then, taking me with him, and then set me on my feet. "Your situation is different from mine."

"You live in a tomb," I pointed out. "Very much as

if you are already dead. Does that serve you in some way?"

"My uncle is my only master," Jovi bit out, but there was something in his gaze when he said it. Something that suggested he chafed at his own words. "He gave me my life and I gave him my soul."

I leaned in and poked a finger into his chest, which was a lot like jabbing it into granite. So I did it again, my gaze fierce on his. "Your soul wasn't his to take."

"You have no idea what you're talking about. Most men in my uncle's position would never have offered me a chance. Most would have killed me with the rest of my family. Instead, he gave me this gift. And what I give him in return is my undying, unquestioning loyalty, until the day I die. It is as simple as that."

Though the way he said it sounded less like a list of unassailable facts than I suspected he knew. "You're the one they send out to the impossible things, aren't you?" I asked.

"They do, because I am the one who is good at them. They require finesse. Patience. Precision." He glared at me. "In a sea of hammers, I am a very sharp knife."

My hands had somehow found my hips. "Or you're the one who doesn't care if he dies, since you've had no reason to live since you were a poor, traumatized boy. No soul. No future. Nothing. Is that really what you're made of, Jovi?"

He blinked. Once. Then his dark eyes blazed. "Please point me in the direction of your agency, Rux. You are a prisoner. I kidnapped you to make you a victim to your father's idiocy, but instead, you offered yourself as a sacrifice. What does that make you?"

But I knew the answer to that. "Yours," I said.

I watched that crash into him. It looked…catastrophic.

"I'm yours, Jovi," I told him, to make sure he heard me. "And if you need me to die for you, I will. If you think your uncle deserves that, too. If you think that's a worthy offering to a man who spared you simply because he could use you, then do it."

And before my eyes, though I could barely credit what I was seeing, I watched this man who never stumbled… stagger back. I watched him put his hands on his head, then tilt back to the blue sky high above.

Then, as I watched, Giovanbattista D'Amato, an impermeable weapon forged of stone and ice, *howled*.

There was no other word for he how he roared. He tipped his head back and what came out was pure anguish.

It went on and on and when he was done, he tipped his head back down. Then he locked eyes with me and everything was *fire*.

"Run," he ordered me, a light in that dark gaze of his that made me breathless.

I didn't think. I could feel that glorious fire burst to life inside me, starting deep between my legs and exploding outward, setting me alight. I turned and threw myself into the overgrown wildness of the garden.

Then I ran. I ran and I ran and it felt mythic. Epic.

I felt like Persephone, running to escape the inevitable while filled with dark excitement I wasn't sure I could admit, even to myself.

I ran as fast and as hard as I could, but he was on me.

He was on me and then we were on the ground, cushioned in a bit of meadow and surrounded on all sides by the wild overgrowth.

Out of sight of that ruined old house and all those ghosts who knew him, too.

Jovi twisted at the last moment so I landed on top of him, his arms were around me, and I was digging my fingers into his skin as our mouths clashed together. It was all anguish and longing, fire and need.

I could feel his hands skimming down my back and then he was grabbing my ass and moving me against him, making sure I could feel the gloriously hard ridge of his cock between my legs.

I remembered the taste of him. I remembered the way he'd gripped my head, held me fast, and plunged deep.

I shuddered at that memory alone, and he muttered something. Then he was busy pulling off the T-shirt I wore so he could haul me up higher against his chest, forcing me onto my hands and knees so he could lavish attention on my breasts.

My hair hung down around us, smelling like a stranger's, and all I could do was make a strange, keening sound I would have told you I wasn't capable of making. It was too raw. Too real.

I could feel myself tightening and gleaming bright. Everything he did to me seemed compounded everywhere else, but before I could crawl my way back down the length of him, he turned me over so that he was on top and it was my turn to move his shirt impatiently out of my way, tearing it over his head and tossing it aside.

Then it was something like awkward, and rushed, as we each clawed at our own trousers, kicking them off and getting them out of our way without losing contact with each other for even a moment.

It was important. It was necessary. It was everything.

And my hands were not the only ones shaking.

He moved over me and, once again, it felt holy. Like we were literally on sacred ground, and I knew, deep down, that there would be no coming back from this.

That the moment I'd seen him, it had always been leading here. That there was no way back.

My old life was as over as if I'd burned it to the ground.

And if I was honest, given gasoline and a match, I might have considered it.

When we were both naked, Jovi settled himself between my thighs. I could feel him against me, the exquisite pressure of his lower body flush against mine, and that gorgeous cock even harder and bigger than I remembered.

He reached between us and I could feel his blunt, hard fingers playing with the softest part of me. He wrapped his hand around his own length, and guided the thick head to my entrance, then he looked at me as he propped himself up on one elbow, his face so fierce it made my heart flip inside my chest. It made a new heat dance all over me.

"Mine," he said, this man of vows.

And I knew this was one of them.

"Yours," I agreed.

And we gazed at each other, consecrating ourselves in this flesh, this earth, this marvel that had found us at the least likely moment.

"I want it to hurt," I told him, ferociously. Almost furiously. "At first. I think it should. I want it to matter."

I felt the shudder that went through him. "You, Ruxandra Emilia Ardelean, are the dream I never had, come true. How is it possible that you could be like this? So perfect it's as if I made you myself."

"Because I'm yours." And then I smiled at him. "Silly."

His eyes gleamed. That would have been enough. But he wasn't done. As I watched, the most dangerous man in the world, naked and on top of me, laughed.

I saw his teeth again. I saw his head tip back. He laughed as if it hurt him a little bit, but he kept going.

And when he looked down at me again, I felt the shock of recognition down into my bones. He might think that I had been made for him. But I knew better. *He* was made for *me*. The key to open all the locks that held me in my whole life. The one weapon forged strong enough to save me, when I had long ago given up on saving myself. When I had accepted that fate would have its way with me, and the best that I could do was wait until it turned its uncompromising eye on someone else.

Jovi was the only man alive who could have taken

me out of there. The only one who would dare, and better yet, could make certain he did it right.

I'd been waiting for him my entire life.

There was still laughter all over his face, but he focused on me and he moved the head of his cock against all my heat, so I could feel him.

And as I opened my mouth to beg him to simply *do it*—

He slammed his way home.

I came all around him, arching up into him, as that searing, impossible pain soared through my body. I felt split in half. I felt like flying. I had never hurt more, and yet even as I thought that, even as the words formed in my head, the pleasure came in behind.

Hotter. Darker.

Fueled by the shock of pain, it went on and on and on, spinning me out, taking me hostage, killing me again and again and again.

And all the while, he waited.

As I slowly shuddered back into my own skin, I could feel him braced above me, murmuring words I couldn't understand. He held himself still, every muscle of his body tense, while he was enormous and rock hard inside me.

I realized that he had only just begun.

"Welcome back, *curò*," he said. And when he traced a shape over my left breast, I thought I knew what it meant. *My heart*.

I felt inside out. I lifted a hand and traced one dark brow, then the other.

"That's a different word. You never told me what the old one meant."

"*Baggiana*," he said. "It means 'foolish woman.' Appropriate, I think you'll agree, but now." He moved inside me, just a little, and we both groaned. "Now I think the time for foolishness is done."

Then he gathered me closer, pulled my legs high over his hips so that I locked my ankles behind his back, and he surged in deep.

He did that a few times, sinking himself inside my body a little more each time. Then pulling himself back. And each time he did it, I could remember the pain of that first thrust less and less.

My body accommodated itself to him. I melted around him as he rocked into me, deeper and deeper, and I was determined to take all of him. I was determined to melt myself completely beneath him.

I knew I had managed it when he began to grunt with each thrust. When his head dropped down as his arms moved beneath us to grab my ass so he was controlling not only his own thrusting but mine, too. Then his mouth was on my throat and I felt him bite, then suck.

I wrapped my arms around his wide shoulders, tipped my head back, and let go.

Because for the first time in all my life, I felt free.

He thrusted harder, deeper. Each time he slammed inside, he scraped against me as he retreated and brought me closer and closer to that edge once again.

Until, finally, I was meeting those magnificent thrusts with the same intensity and we were both slicked with sweat, determined and mad with the same need that was in us both.

"You are mine, Rux," he intoned, dark and forbidding, there at my ear. "You will always be mine, as long as we live. This I promise you."

"You are mine," I told him in return, though I could barely speak and I could hear my breathlessness in my voice. "You are always and ever mine. Always, Jovi."

And on the next thrust, he turned me into fireworks.

Then, with a shout, he followed me into all those pyrotechnics.

I could feel him deep inside me, as if he belonged there. As if the entire purpose of our bodies was this joining, this melting, and the spectacular explosions that went on and on and on.

Even as I could feel that scalding heat of his, flooding me from within.

At some point, many centuries removed, or perhaps a few moments, he disengaged from me and laughed again when I made a small sound of loss.

Jovi was astonishingly beautiful naked, with the sun playing all over his body. He looked like a god, here on this island that I suspected had seen its share of them in its time. He looked like he'd stepped out of a myth when he reached down and hauled me up into his arms again, then carried me back into that ruined old house, up the stairs, and inside.

He didn't take me to the room I'd woken up in, but led me in a different direction entirely, sweeping into a room on the other side of the house that I knew at once was his. There was what looked like a wardrobe in one corner, and the bed had a bed frame. Both exquisitely wrought. But I only registered those tiny hints of actual furnishings before he took me into a bathroom suite and directly into a shower that had been built for an army.

As the water beat down all around us, he lathered me with soap, seeming to check every part of my body as he did it. Particularly the back of me and the bottoms of my feet, and it occurred to me after a moment that he was making certain that our run to the garden hadn't hurt me.

I didn't know how to tell him that I would have preferred it if I was as scarred as he was. If everything we did together left a mark so that I could display it to the world.

He squeezed shampoo into his cupped hand, then massaged it into my hair.

I leaned back against him as he worked. "You watched me while I was sleeping, too."

"I did."

"Since the beginning, you've taken care with me. Do you know why?"

I didn't think he was going to answer. He rinsed out my hair, focusing on his task with a certain determination, and yet when he was done, he turned me back to face him. He slicked the water back from my face.

"You make me want to protect you," he told me, as if it was a dark confession. "I don't know why. That is not something I know how to do."

"You do know how," I argued, with too much emotion all over me. "And you're good at it."

"Such an irony," he murmured.

It was my turn to advance on him, and I did. I pushed him back against the tile wall and tilted my head up as I leaned in.

"Listen to me," I demanded, fiercely. "A weapon is nothing more than a tool. You can decide how to use it. You can decide whether you draw blood or build something better. You don't owe your soul to anyone, Jovi."

I reached over and put my hand on this tattoo. I traced it with my fingers, then I leaned close and kissed it, too. "I can feel your heart beating. As long as I can, that means you're alive. And you belong to *you*, no matter what your uncle told you. No matter what he made you. You can choose to be anything you want."

He stared at me, then he made a noise I couldn't interpret. He reached over and slapped off the water, then he led me from the shower. He seemed almost brusque and impatient as he toweled me off, but then he led me back into the bedroom and sat on his bed, taking me down with him.

He hooked his palm on the back of my neck and pulled me close to kiss him as I straddled him.

After a while, deep and wild, he pulled his mouth away. His hands on my hips, he repositioned me over his cock and let me find the right fit. I looked down at his impossible male beauty as I lifted myself up, then found my seat again. Finding myself impaled anew each time.

Just like before, he let me do as I would until something shifted inside him, his grip on my hips changed, and he took over.

The truth was, as much as I liked playing, I liked it when he took charge of me even more.

Jovi taught me how to ride him, and I did. I arched into him and I surrendered myself into his grip, once again, until we touched the sky and shattered into pieces.

Together.

But when I woke up, he was gone.

CHAPTER TEN

LEAVING RUX IN his bed, alone, was the hardest thing Jovi had ever done.

She had drifted off to sleep but he hadn't dozed off with her. He'd stayed awake, sprawled out beside her, the soft weight of her curled up at his side.

The kind of thing that had always horrified him to imagine, which was why he had never allowed it. But it was Rux.

Everything was different.

She had called him a protector. She had claimed he was good at it. He had wanted to tell her she could not possibly have been more wrong, but that would have involved talking about the very deepest memories inside him that he did his best to keep at bay.

Though it was harder now. Something about Rux made him wonder if he'd ever truly banished his memories. Because now it seemed patently obvious that he hadn't. That they'd been waiting here for him all along.

He remembered trying to block the closet where his sisters had hidden, imagining that he could save them. He remembered the screaming from somewhere else in the villa, and had spent most of his life choosing not to know who had been doing it. Yet he could still hear it so clearly. He could still *feel it* inside him, if he allowed it.

It had been his own uncle who had clubbed him across the head. There had been two shots, then Antonio had stared down at him, pitiless.

Am I going to have to take care of you too, you little shit? he'd asked. This man whose lap Jovi had napped in when he was smaller. This man who usually ruffled his head and gave him extra dessert at the family table. He had known it was Antonio, but that night, his uncle had looked like a monster. Something out of the nightmares Jovi had thought he should have been too old to keep having. *Or can I make you useful to me?*

Jovi hadn't said a word. He'd had blood in his mouth. His ears were ringing, but at least he couldn't hear any more screaming. He'd wanted to cry.

He'd known better.

Smart kid, Antonio had said. *Keep your mouth shut, unlike your* stronzo *father.*

Then he'd kicked Jovi in the stomach, for good measure, before he'd had his men drag him out of the house. They'd thrown him in the back of their car and had delivered him, unceremoniously, to his uncle's house. He'd been kept in a tiny room at the back, visited only by his angry aunt, and it hadn't been until many years later that he'd realized his life had likely been in the balance that whole time.

It had only been after a few weeks of keeping Jovi locked away had his uncle decided that he would, in fact, create a secret weapon to unleash on his enemies. Before that, his nephew had been considered "missing"—and at any point, Antonio could have killed him, too.

That wasn't a realization Jovi liked to revisit.

This was exactly why Jovi kept these things out of his head. This was why he had never let another human close to him, because closeness led to blood.

Though if he was entirely honest with himself, he doubted that there was any other person on earth who could have gotten to him like this, so far under his skin that he had no choice but to revisit…everything that had led him here. To her.

So he'd held Rux close in his bed, baffled that urge to do so seemed to be more a *physical need* than anything else. He'd stared at the ceiling in this haunted place, and had been deeply pleased that he'd had the place stripped down. He didn't think he would have been able to handle the memories that poked at him if he hadn't. If his father's books were still overflowing from their shelves. If his mother's paintings still graced the walls. If his sisters' toys were left as they had been, in and around the bin in their playroom—

Stop, he had ordered himself.

He had pushed the memories away—though he was aware, then, that they didn't go anywhere. That he could no longer cut them off from himself. But instead of lingering on the implications of that, he had set about meticulously plotting out his next move.

And the one after that. And on and on, testing strategies in his head, throwing in different obstacles, and revising as he went.

But no matter how he'd approached the problem,

he'd arrived at the same conclusion. There was only one way out of this. And he doubted very much that it would be anything but painful.

He hadn't been surprised—maybe he was even proud—that Rux was worn out, so he'd let her keep sleeping. While she did, he'd slipped out of the bed, showered once again, and then tended to some business that he could not accomplish electronically.

It took the better part of the afternoon.

When he came back, he found her dressed in the clothes he'd torn off her in the garden. She was sitting out on the back steps, looking pensive.

"Where have you been?" she asked. She did not sound accusatory. Jovi almost wanted her to, so he could perhaps convince himself that she was just a woman like any other.

"Surely you're hungry," he said, instead of answering her question.

She looked up at him as if she was trying to read him and his instant response to that was to make himself impassive, a wall of blank stone, to keep her out. The way he kept everyone out.

It took a significant effort to stop doing that, and it made him...not exactly *angry*. He didn't allow himself anger. But he didn't wish to discover what else it could have been. He just knew he didn't like it.

"You don't always have to feed me, you know," Rux told him with great seriousness, her gaze dark gray and deeply grave. "You don't always have to tend to me like I can't take care of myself."

Jovi studied her. He liked the way the breeze played

with her hair. He liked the way she curled around herself as she sat. "But I want to."

He watched her melt in real time, and so it was a little longer, then, before he took her into the kitchen and satisfied himself by serving her the pasta he made and then insisted she eat until she was full.

First he had needed to taste her all over again, to be sure.

This was a pattern that repeated itself as the days passed, one into the next, like something from a dream. The sun was so bright. The sea beckoned from afar. The mountain rose strong and tall, and the birds sang them arias to while away their days.

It was almost like a holiday, if Jovi ignored the many things he was putting in place.

If he ignored the storm that drew closer to them by the moment, and was likely to eat them whole.

"How long do you think we have?" Rux asked one night, tucked up against him in bed.

Jovi had just taken her with a ferocity that should have shocked him, but this was his Rux. Whatever he brought to her, she met it and gave it back. She had teased him, and it had taken him a moment to understand both that she was teasing him—actually *teasing* him—and that he'd liked it.

But he had punished her all the same. He'd turned her over his lap, spanking her lightly to make her laugh. Then harder, to make her moan, before he'd thrown her over the side of the bed and taken her roughly from behind.

His reward for that had been the way she'd clenched

all around him, trembling wildly and crying out her pleasure. And then again, when he'd flipped her over onto her sore ass and taken her again.

That was where they'd both discovered something he'd suspected all along. That what she really liked was discipline. That second time she'd started coming and hadn't stopped, bright red everywhere with his name in her mouth while he'd pounded into her.

His beautiful Rux.

That ache in his chest hurt all the time now. He'd stopped concerning himself with it. If it was a mortal wound, he imagined it would have killed him by now. Like everything else that had tried, he intended to best it.

He didn't pretend not to understand her question. *How long do we have?*

Both of them knew that whatever they were doing here, it was all on borrowed time. That fact—the truth of who he was and who she was and what that meant to people and organizations that extended far beyond a haunted old villa in Sicily—was inescapable.

And the longer they were not discovered, the more likely it was that when they were, the price they would pay for breaking all the rules would be that much higher.

He should have known that Rux was as keenly aware of this as he was.

"Your father is searching for you and he becomes more unhinged the longer it takes without any sign of you, as it reflects badly on his ability to control his little empire," he told her, baldly. "He has enlisted a number of unsavory individuals to aid him in his search, but while he first suspected that you ran off with one of your guards—"

"I hope I am never *that much* of a cliché," Rux sniffed.

"—he has now come to think that there is more than meets the eye when it comes to your disappearance."

He felt the pattern she was tracing across his chest, found her hand, and held it fast.

"This is because you didn't do what you said you would do, isn't it?" When he didn't respond, she looked up at him. "Wasn't I meant to beg and plead? Throw myself on his mercy? Make it all very clear what was happening?"

Things she had not done because she had cast her spell on him instead.

"Perhaps because he has been left to come up with his own theories, your father is starting to make wild accusations." Jovi shrugged, though he was not nearly as unbothered as he wanted her to think. "This alone will cause him trouble."

Her gaze seemed to pin him in place, as if she knew precisely how bothered they both were by the reality of their situation, no matter what they chose not to say to each other during their sleepy, sunny days. "He always thinks the Russians are after him. They never are."

"More worrying is the inevitability that his search will make its way to Sicily," he told her quietly. "And when."

"Surely your uncle—"

But Jovi did not want to talk about his uncle. Not yet.

So he kissed her instead. He built up that heat.

He distracted them both as best he could.

It took a few more days for him to put certain precautions into place, and to finesse a few of the more tedious, bureaucratic issues in play. It was tempting to question why he was doing such a thing in the first place when it would be infinitely easier to stop. And to do what he'd been ordered to do.

But then every time he came back to the villa, he found he lost himself more and more in Rux. And the way she came running to meet him, once—at his request—she ascertained that it was actually him. He did not like to think what would happen if someone else came by and saw her here.

Some mornings she would wake before he did and he would find her out in the garden wandering in and out of the overgrown rows, as if she was familiarizing herself with all of that green, all of that bloom. Sometimes he would find her on one of the balconies that faced the sea, looking out at the birds flying high over all that blue as if she wished she could take flight herself.

As if she'd never seen too much of the world, just the cells that had held her.

He could not think on that too much or he might find a reason to return to that ugly fortress in Prague to express his thoughts on that to Boris Ardelean directly.

Jovi had come to accept, however begrudgingly, that while he did not enjoy surrendering himself to his feelings—having only recently accepted that he possessed them—there were some things that took him over, and she was one of them.

She was all of them, if he was honest.

One evening they were out in the garden. It was a mild night, and the sea air was soft against his face as he sat beneath his favorite tree, smiling—yes, actually *smiling*—because Rux was acting out her favorite movie for him.

She had asked if he'd watched it. He had assured her that he had no interest in entertainment and besides, he did not keep electronic devices around this house. There was only his tablet and his mobile. Nothing else.

Don't tell me that at heart you're a Luddite, she'd said, clucking her tongue.

She was wearing one of the dresses he'd bought her, something shimmery and bright that reminded him of her laughter. He liked to see her in it. He liked to hear her laugh. He particularly liked to make her laugh when he was deep inside her and could *feel* her laughter, like he was learning how to be something more than ice by feeling her do it.

But this was no longer that first night and the glut of need thereafter. There was no longer the same driving requirement to take her in a wild rush, knowing that he would lose her by his own hand, and soon.

It was possible that even if he tried such a thing now, his own hands would defy him and do as they liked. Which could never involve hurting her in any way that did not involve the bedroom.

These days he could allow the anticipation to build. He could actually let himself enjoy it. He could *feel*, which was something he certainly wasn't comfortable with, but he was willing to do it.

Around Rux only.

Electronic devices can be hacked, he told her. *The fewer I have, the less likely it is that they will be compromised. And the more easily I can monitor them on the off chance that someone imagines they might best me.*

She'd eyed him for a moment and he'd braced himself, imagining that would be one of her quiet questions that he always interpreted as an attack. That was what it felt like—as if she was taking a sword she should not have been able to wield and slamming it straight to his ribs, through to that place where his heart still ached.

But she didn't ask him anything. Instead, she started acting out the movie—something involving a princess named after a flower and her romantic travails.

The strangest part was, he was actually enjoying it.

Jovi found anything and everything she did charming. That was the issue.

And he was already deciding how best he would reward this charm, what level of obedience he would require, and how many times he would use it to make her melt in his hands. He liked a challenge, after all. Particularly one *she* felt was impossible.

But instead, he heard the sound of a familiar car on his drive, and everything…splintered.

He was no longer made of ice, perhaps, but he was still him.

And he didn't need to go and see who, precisely, was approaching the villa. Time was up no matter who it was.

Suddenly, the time they'd had until now seemed like a blink. A moment.

When Rux froze, her gaze on him, he realized she was mimicking whatever he was doing. He didn't have to tell her not to speak, to let him listen. She knew enough to simply watch him and wait.

Everything in him stilled, the way he'd taught himself long ago.

He heard a car door slam, but only the one. He knew it could only be one person—the one who would scoff at the notion that he needed henchmen no matter what he was doing, but who would also have been forced to bring them along if he'd come to do something himself.

That meant that Antonio was extending an invitation to his nephew.

Jovi let himself work through the various chess moves that this opening salvo on the family's part put into play, then moved his gaze back to Rux.

Who stood there waiting, God help him, as if she would wait for him forever.

"Go into the garden," he told her, and did nothing to make his voice less dark. "Hide yourself well and don't come out. Not until I tell you to."

He thought she might argue, but she didn't. She only whirled around, and darted into that undergrowth. He watched her go and noted exactly where she disappeared, crouching down into a gnarled section that looked like thorns.

Good girl, he thought.

He picked up the tray of *friscu* and *arancina* and tossed it all into the greenery, so that it would not look as if he was entertaining anything but his usual grim thoughts.

And when his cousin made his way out of the house and down the back stairs, Jovi looked the way he always did.

Sitting still beneath the tree, gazing at nothing. Doing nothing.

Although this time, it was clear to Jovi that he'd lost his touch. He was no longer the man of ice he been his whole life. He was well and truly melted. But he could not allow himself to worry about that. He thought of ice. Stone.

More than that, he thought of what would happen if Carlo had any reason to suspect him. Of anything.

It didn't matter if he *felt* like ice, he reminded himself. Only that he *looked* like it.

As usual, he did not greet his cousin until Carlo had come around to stand over him, looming in that way of his that he no doubt imagined was threatening—though with his coward's inability to follow through without already knowing he had the upper hand.

"How long have you been back?" Carlo asked. Perhaps he imagined it came out as a threatening demand, but he couldn't seem to stand still.

Jovi cut his gaze to his cousin and remained impassive. He did not clear his schedule through Carlo. He never had and he never would.

It occurred to him that Rux had not been wrong to suggest that he had a kind of death wish. He served his uncle. He would not serve his cousin. There was only one way that typically ended.

Had he always known that? Or had he simply not cared enough to think through the details and possibilities?

It was amazing what clarity a man could find when his heart finally beat properly in his chest. So loudly that he was shocked his cousin couldn't hear it, but then, he doubted Carlo heard much above the din of his own self-interest.

Carlo looked at him, then quickly away when he accidentally met Jovi's gaze. "My father wants to talk to you. You can't be surprised."

"I am neither surprised nor unsurprised," Jovi replied without inflection. "That is not my job."

"Your job was to take that bitch out," Carlo retorted. "Instead—"

"Instead?" Jovi asked. Mildly. "Have you laid eyes on her? Has anyone?"

Carlo scowled him, but he didn't dare maintain eye contact. Jovi merely gazed back at him.

For a long moment, there was nothing. The sea air. The night sky.

"He wants to see you now," Carlo gritted out. "Unless you have some compelling reason why you're suddenly disobeying orders?"

Jovi stood. He did it smoothly and swiftly, and managed not to smile when his cousin stepped back. Quickly.

"Are you questioning my loyalty, Carlo?" he asked in the same mild way he always did, complete with a faint tilt of his head.

He was well aware that the effect on others was threatening.

Carlo shook his head, temper and fear all over his face. "Just remember, my father takes promises seriously."

It was almost as if he was warning Jovi. Helping him.

Almost.

What Jovi remembered was that Carlo had been here in the villa that night, though he'd been a boy himself. He remembered his cousin's gleeful expression. His high-pitched laughter, more disturbing than the screaming—and not any better when Jovi could no longer hear him.

He'd blocked that out for a long time, because it wasn't helpful.

Jovi merely gazed back at Carlo until the other man shifted again, clearly uncomfortable. And likely furious that it showed. That his cowardice flashed neon bright and Jovi had never pretended he couldn't see it.

"I never forget it," Jovi assured him in the same soft tone. "I never will."

He didn't look back toward the garden. He kept his gaze trained on his cousin. "There is only one person who deserves my loyalty. And it has never been you, *cucinu*."

Carlo made a noise at that, as if he couldn't believe Jovi dared. But not a loud noise, because he knew better. Behind him, Jovi thought he heard a rustle in the shrubbery, though he didn't dare look to see. He could not allow himself to be the one who gave Rux away.

"Take your own car. I'm not a taxi service," Carlo muttered, trying to make it sound like the potential for inconvenience was the reason he didn't want to be in a vehicle with Jovi. Not the more practical concern, which was that Jovi could easily overpower him and be rid of him in short order. They both knew it.

Maybe, Jovi realized now, this had always been a power struggle that he'd never bothered to play.

Maybe he'd hoped his cousin would do something about it, because whatever happened would have been fine with the Jovi who felt nothing at all but cold.

But that Jovi was gone now.

"I will follow you there," he assured his cousin. "I might even beat you."

Carlo obviously took that as a challenge, wheeling around and taking off toward his car.

Jovi almost turned back to take one last look in Rux's direction, but he couldn't let himself do it. It was time to be finished with this, once and for all.

Looking at her would only make it impossible to do what needed to be done.

He followed his cousin out at a far more measured pace, swinging into his car and noting the clouds of dust his cousin had kicked up behind him in his haste to win over Jovi in the only meaningless way he could. As if that mattered.

As if any part of this corrupt life mattered.

Jovi took his time driving through Palermo, accepting as he did that it was very unlikely he would ever see it again. The wild mountains, the ancient ruins.

The hardy, independent people who had made him who he was.

He was proud he'd lived as long as he had a Sicilian to his core.

Antonio's house was on the other side of the city, a seemingly modest affair at the end of a cracked and barely paved road. If, that was, a visitor ignored the views of the bay and the sea beyond. Or was unaware that all the buildings a person could see from his uncle's front door were, in fact, also his. Outbuildings, warehouses, and sometimes even a place to visit a mistress or two. Antonio did precisely what he wished, when he wished it, as his father had before him.

When Jovi pulled up to the house, he saw that Carlo's car was already parked haphazardly near the fountain in front. Instead of walking in the front door, he left his car near one of the garages and ducked around the side, nodding at the guards he saw along the way, and then letting himself in one of the doors near the back of the house.

It was always best to disrupt any potential ambush scenarios.

He made his way through the kitchen, which was quiet this time of night. And he found himself near the back room where his uncle had stashed him years ago. Jovi paused, then followed an urge that he could barely fathom to push open that door.

The room was empty. It was more of a closet than a room, to his eye. It still had a mattress on the floor, which was all he'd been allowed, and what barely passed for a window cut high in the wall—more of a vent, really.

This was where his uncle and aunt had kept him. This was where they had thrown food in through the door and made him do his business in a pail in the corner that he'd had to clean out himself.

The memories came back at him like gunfire. A hail of bullets, each one slamming into him hard.

The things they'd made him do, because it amused them to debase him.

Things he had learned to handle with that blankness, that ice.

Because, deep down, he knew that it was the only weapon he really had. The only one that got to them. It was what had convinced his uncle to let him live.

But only because Antonio had imagined he could control it.

Jovi shook off the memories, though his chest felt as if he'd been riddled with bullets. He could feel the agony of it like a blaze—but that wasn't a bad thing.

Pain, he'd learned right here in this room, was clarifying. It brought the world into sharp focus. It made sense of things that otherwise seemed fuzzy and confusing.

The pain of what had happened here to the boy he'd been fueled him. It protected him.

It allowed him to step back out into the hall and make his way into the main part of the house.

Where he could hear his cousin's voice, shouting already.

Jovi thought that boded well. It meant he'd succeeded in getting into Carlo's head.

He made his way down the hall, inclined his head at the guard that stood outside his uncle's study, and didn't argue when the man indicated that he had to be searched. He submitted to the brisk pat down impassively. It was standard procedure if anyone wanted to get to see Don Antonio.

If he'd been anyone but Antonio's nephew, he wouldn't have walked into the house so easily. They would have taken him down before he made it up the drive and asked questions later.

When he was pronounced clean, Jovi let himself inside.

"I could hear you yelling all the way down the hall," he said to his cousin, sounding something almost like pleasant. He looked at his uncle. "As ever, I congratulate you on your coolheaded successor."

Carlo looked as if he wanted to lunge at Jovi. Or use the weapon he didn't have to relinquish, because he was the *sotto capo*.

But he didn't. Because he was only and ever a coward where it counted.

Antonio, on the other hand, merely studied Jovi, all cold assessment. "Interesting approach," he said after a moment, and it wasn't a compliment. Because while he often complained about his son, it was a risk for anyone else to insult him by doing the same. "What happened to that girl in Prague?"

Jovi stared back at this man who had been a shadow

over his whole life. The man who had literally kicked Jovi while he was down. Repeatedly.

The older man had gotten rounder as the years had gone by. Gravity had not been kind to his face. Or his spine, though Jovi accepted the possibility that he was the one who had grown tall. Maybe his uncle had always been much smaller than he acted.

Not that his size did anything to dilute the depraved power that emanated from Antonio.

"What do you think happened to that girl?" he asked him. He kept his back to the door and fixed his gaze on his uncle. "Am I normally in the habit of disobeying you, *Ziu*?"

"I hope not," Antonio said with that laugh of his that made many a man's bowels fail him. He didn't have to infuse his voice with any further threat.

The threat was him. The threat was this house. The threat was Jovi's entire life up to this moment.

But Jovi felt all those bullets, all those memories, and stood tall.

"Yet you question my work?" Jovi asked. He looked at his uncle as he said it, then swung his gaze to his cousin. "Do you, Carlo?"

Carlo looked as if he wanted to start shouting, raging, brandishing his weapon—but he didn't. Antonio merely studied his nephew some more. Longer than was comfortable.

And after a while, he nodded his head toward the door. "Get out," he told Carlo. "And calm yourself down while you're at it. You're turning red like a *picciriddu*."

The look Carlo threw Jovi was murderous, not that Jovi cared. His cousin *was* acting like a baby boy. He only wondered why his uncle made it sound as if that was something other than business as usual where Carlo was concerned.

Jovi stepped out of the way as Carlo barreled toward him, and for a moment he thought his cousin was going to try to tackle him—

But at the very last moment, Carlo thought better of it.

What a shock, Jovi thought, and was certain the sentiment showed on his face.

When the door closed behind him, louder than it should have, Antonio waved to the seat near his preferred armchair, where he liked to lounge like he was a king on a throne.

Here in Sicily, he was.

But Jovi shook his head.

"What is this?" his uncle asked quietly.

Dangerously.

Jovi looked at Antonio for a long while. He remembered the boy he had been, scared and grieving—and beaten for both. He remembered the grim years spent under this roof, the man he'd had to make himself into to survive it, and what it had cost him to become the version of himself he was now.

Or had been, before Rux had turned all that heat and light of hers upon him, and melted all his ice away.

Year after year, his uncle had stripped Jovi down and built him back up into exactly the kind of monster he needed to do his dirtiest work.

Until he was so deep in the ice it was as if his veins were frozen solid, too, because that was the only possible way to survive.

But now he could feel the blood in him, the heat.

He could hear his own heartbeat, even here in the most dangerous place he'd ever been—the place he'd first learned, long ago, to hide it and anything else that made him human.

He looked at his uncle and tried to see if it was visible on his face. If there was any clue to the brutality this man could dish out without a second thought. This man who had murdered his own brother and his brother's wife and young daughters. This man who had brought his own son along and treated a bloodbath like a party.

This man who had then made sure that the only survivor of that night paid for his father's sins by becoming a creature who would have been Donatello's worst nightmare.

Because that was the real reason Antonio had kept him alive.

Donatello had been too gentle for this life, too academic. He'd been horrified by the violence and the sadistic pleasure Antonio took in it.

So Antonio had not only killed him, he'd stolen his son's soul, too.

Simply because he could.

And that was only a little glimpse into the horrors that Antonio D'Amato had visited upon the world.

That was only what Jovi's uncle had done to *him*. It barely scratched the surface of the things Antonio was capable of. It would hardly register on the laundry list of offenses the police likely attributed to him.

"Do you remember my sister Alessia?" he asked his uncle.

"Have you lost your mind?" Antonio asked with that laugh of his, his eyes cold. "You want to get into ancient history?"

"Either one of my sisters, actually. Alessia or Isabella." Jovi watched his uncle's face. "I can barely remember them myself. They were so little. But then, I don't really remember my mother, either."

Though he did, now. He remembered her voice that night, defying Antonio's orders and calling him exactly what he was. A daring act that had cost her dearly, but she'd done it.

"Your mother was a whore," Antonio told him, with obvious relish. "Does that clear it up? Can we get back to business now?"

What Jovi knew about his mother was that she'd been from Rome. Educated and artistic, she'd never really fit in with the family. *Uppity*, his aunt had sneered. Jovi remembered her art. Her dancing in a pretty dress.

Maybe he was protecting himself from all the other things he couldn't bear to remember.

But one thing he was sure of was that his mother was no whore.

So what Jovi did in the face of such slander was smile.

And he saw that when he did, he managed to disconcert his uncle more than any flash of temper might have. Antonio understood temper. He banked on it. He liked to force others into violent displays because it made it easier to then take what he wanted.

He'd never known what to do with the monster he'd made, a creature of ice instead of fury.

It was time, Jovi thought, that he found out.

CHAPTER ELEVEN

I STAYED CROUCHED down behind that bush for a long time. I stayed while my legs cramped and my knees ached—

But convent girls were bred to endure. We'd been taught how to suffer, and we'd practiced it in prayer day and night in wildly uncomfortable old buildings that had never known any creature comforts.

I had literally spent my life preparing for this moment.

I stayed in place, tucked up under bush that had managed to grow into something thick with thorns, providing me with something like a cocoon. I pulled my dress around me and pretended it was a blanket. I curled up and hunkered down, determined to wait it out.

And absolutely certain that Jovi would make it back to me, because I could accept no other outcome.

But eventually, it began to get colder. Darker. The night was wearing on and I'd heard nothing to suggest that there was anyone on this property but me.

Despite the fact that Jovi had told me to stay put, I crept out of my little burrow. I stopped again and again, scouring the dark for any sign of life. In my experience, guards and other such people had a lot of nervous energy. They paced. They smoked cigarettes and flicked them. They were very concerned with perimeters and constantly went to recheck them.

I melted my way through the overgrowth, careful to keep my steps silent, and when I got to Jovi's tree, I stopped and waited some more. But all I could hear was the wind, and every now and then, the faintest sound of the city far below.

If there was someone here, I reasoned, he would have to be even more still and watchful than Jovi.

This being impossible to imagine, I used the darkness to my advantage. I snuck around the side of the house to make sure there were no other cars in the drive. I checked all the balconies from the shadows below.

Then I went inside. I padded up to Jovi's bedroom, where I'd stayed ever since that first day. I opened up the wardrobe and breathed in the faint scent of him on his clothes, then pulled on a pair of denim so soft it was like a whisper and a sweater, because I'd started shivering. He had showed me the stack of clothes he kept in what looked like a gym bag early on—maybe the second morning I'd been here—and told me they were all mine.

You just happened to have clothing in my size lying about, of course, I'd murmured.

I bought them for you only, baggiana, he had replied, sounding as close to outraged as I'd ever heard him.

And I had melted all over him before I'd had a chance to try any of them on.

Unsurprisingly, everything he'd chosen fit me perfectly, because Jovi paid attention to details. He'd assembled an elegant collection of very few, but very sophisticated, pieces and had told me with a frown that it was only temporary.

By that point I hadn't wanted to ask if he'd meant it would be temporary because I would be dying soon.

I'd suspected he wouldn't like it if I had asked.

Now I found the presence of the clothes comforting. Or maybe it was just that they shared a wardrobe with his. I hugged my arms around my own middle and tried to make sense of what I'd seen and heard.

The truth was, lovely clothes or not, I had an unpleasant pit in my stomach.

Because it seemed to me that Jovi had gone off with his horrible cousin much too easily, and I couldn't think why he would do that.

I'd spent hours in my burrow asking myself why he would surrender himself so easily.

And the only conclusion I'd reached made me shake.

This was a man with a death wish. Hadn't I told him so myself?

This was a man who would, I was absolutely certain, sacrifice himself to save me without a second thought. A man who would protect me with everything he had, even if it was his final act.

That asshole.

I wanted him to come back so I could kill him myself.

I wanted *him*, not some noble act that would leave me alone in this life without him.

When only he knew me, and where I came from, and what it meant to grow up in this dark and terrible world.

When he'd finally showed me his heart.

I wanted *him*.

Too many scenes played out in my head and they all made me sick. I knew exactly what men like his family were capable of. I knew what they thought was fun. What they considered a reasonable response to disloyalty.

I didn't want to think about such things. I didn't want to picture them happening to Jovi—or to me, if they found me after they dealt with him. But I stood in this bedroom we shared, here in this ruined old house, this graveyard of despair and loss.

I was surrounded by his ghosts and he knew their names, but all I knew was that they all died horribly. That it was likely I would, too. That all the beauty of this house couldn't change the fact that the ghost stories told about it were right.

It was haunted. This island was haunted. And anyone who ventured near this life was tainted and ruined, and marked for their own bad end.

Though not all of them walked into that end as calmly as Jovi had.

I found myself wandering through the creaky old house the way I had that first day. I didn't turn on any lights, still too aware that there could be eyes on me, but the moon was bright enough outside to light my way. I traced my fingers over the bare walls. I stood and watched the moonlight dance across the halls.

It was so tempting to imagine that the ghosts here were Jovi, and if I loved him enough, I could free them and him and me in turn.

I didn't know if I was relieved or embarrassed to finally admit that little tidbit to myself. So obvious. So *immediate*.

And probably very, very stupid, too.

Eventually I made it down into his kitchen, chased by all the images in my head that I didn't want to see. All the things that could be happening to him *right now*.

I felt my knees give out beneath me and had to clutch at the counter to keep myself from sagging straight down to the floor.

At first I thought I was having some kind of heart attack. Or aneurysm. It wasn't until my eyes started to mist over and then get wet that I realized I was crying.

I wiped at my face, astonished, but the tears didn't stop.

Neither did the pain in my chest. Because it turned out that it was called *heartbreak* for a reason, and I'd had no idea.

I'd had no idea that it could hurt this much.

I'd had no idea *anything* could.

But I couldn't bear the notion that he was hurting. Or that he would consider that a decent trade, because he likely imagined that his death would set me free.

I couldn't *bear* this.

When I'd met him, I'd been resigned to this. I hadn't

been as scared as I thought a normal girl would have been, plucked out of her safe life and carried off by a man like Jovi. I'd already been well aware that nothing about my life was safe.

If I couldn't have a good life, what I'd wanted was a good death. I thought that I could walk into my execution, head held high, and that would mean something.

I understood exactly what Jovi was doing, damn him.

But I hadn't known anything yet. I hadn't *lived* yet.

Tonight I didn't think I had a single ounce of resignation in me. I didn't want a death, good or otherwise. I wanted a life. I wanted *this* life, strange as it was, because I'd been so sure it was *ours*.

I wanted to *live*.

With him.

I wanted the fact that we'd met the way we had to *mean something*—to prove that we had always been destined to be better, to shine brighter, than the people who'd made us who we were.

God, how desperately I wanted that.

I wiped my face, again and again, until the tears released their hold on me. I tried to breathe. I tried to settle myself the way I'd always been able to before. And I was still standing there, staring into the shadows of the sink, when I heard a soft noise behind me.

In the same instant, the kitchen was flooded with light.

I whirled around, not sure what I expected. His cousin, back to finish the job? That would mean that Jovi—

I couldn't bear it—

But it was Jovi himself.

And I couldn't tell if I was relieved or something far more complicated.

Or maybe, despite myself, both.

I backed up and hit the counter, so I rested my hands on either side of my body as if I couldn't decide if I wanted to launch myself into the air to sit on the countertop, or hold myself upright.

Jovi merely stood there, studying me, the way he always did.

That made the ache inside me worse.

I could feel that unbearable weight inside me. I could see all those horrific images that I'd played in my mind, all the ways they could have killed him.

Asshole, I thought again.

"Are you going to kill me now?" I asked him, because maybe he should see what it felt like to think that everything that happened between us was easy to walk away from. Maybe he should feel as alone as I had. "I thought you went to fulfill your death wish, but maybe what you really wanted was more detailed instructions from your keeper."

He seemed to freeze at that. Then something dark moved in his gaze, making me immediately feel terrible for lashing out at him. For trying to scare him because he'd scared me.

For treating him like the man I knew he wasn't.

But I didn't take it back.

"This is what I am good for," he told me, with a certain deliberateness that made me want to run and throw myself into his arms. It made me want to press my lips to all the places he hurt, starting with his heart. "Haven't I said this to you before? I am a weapon. A monster. I was made precisely for the purpose I serve. I am the very model of efficiency and promise."

"So you keep saying," I managed to reply.

He moved into the kitchen then, prowling his way toward me. Behind him, I could see the light spill out into the empty rooms of this place, all of them graceful, exquisite.

Pointless, standing empty like this.

A lot like the man he pretended he was. But I knew better.

Did he?

"So what happens?" I asked, watching him closely. "If you kill me, who cares? I'm an unremarkable casualty. My father, despite his outsized sense of self-importance, matters to no one. I doubt very much anyone will notice when he's gone."

His eyes flared with an emotion I recognized, because I'd felt it myself moments before when he'd declared that this was all he was good for, all he was. These ghosts. This violence. This grotesque mirror of what life *should* have been.

"My uncle does not need your father gone just yet," he said coolly, as if he'd never been inside me. So deep I'd forgotten we had separate names. So deep I'd seen forever. But I knew him better now. I knew that the colder he got, the less he truly believed what he was saying. I kept my gaze on his face. I watched his eyes that were no longer ice-cold, but bright. "He needs him neutralized. Humbled. But then he prefers everyone in that position. The more bowing and scraping, the better."

I nodded. "You would know how to do that best, of course."

He made his way deeper into the kitchen, and his gaze was fastened on me as if he couldn't decide if he wanted to kiss me or kill me after all.

"I find humbling myself overrated," Jovi told me, darkly.

He kept coming, and I wondered why he couldn't hear how hard my heart was pounding. Why he couldn't read me the way I read him. I might have asked him, but then he was right in front of me.

And he leaned forward, putting his hands on either side of me, directly beside mine. Then he was leaning onto the counter, towering over me while I was staring up at him in what I hoped looked like defiance.

But the only thing I was really defying, I thought, was my own very real urge to throw myself into his arms. Because I wanted to see what he would say. What he would do. What value he put on the trust I'd thought we had between us—until he went off to court his probable death.

"Tell me what you think is happening here," Jovi said, and he sounded…impatient and dark. Dangerous and something like *indulgent*, if an indulgence could be that hard. "And make it quick. We are short on time, you and me."

"What's *time* between a killer and his victim?" I asked airily, as if I was still that girl who he'd carried out of my father's house, bound and gagged and yet held securely and kept warm on the way out.

He muttered something beneath his breath. "*Baggiana*, I have told you. I am a man of vows."

"I know that," I fired back at him. "And yet you continue to honor your cruel, vicious uncle for some reason, even after he slaughtered your family and forced you to be a monster just like him—"

"I blocked out my memories of my family," Jovi gritted out at me, standing so close I thought we might as well have been touching, his gaze so intense on mine. "It was better this way. It allowed me to function. It allowed me to survive." He shook his head, though his dark gaze never left mine. "I was always taught that my father was a weak man. A small man, greedy and vain. But I remember now."

I wanted, desperately, to touch him. I whispered his name instead.

Jovi swallowed. "He was neither. He wanted something better. Something clean. He wanted to save his family from this greed and horror that my uncle would tell you is in our blood. My father wanted to cut it out. He wanted to leave. But every time he thought about how he would do that, how he would convince Antonio to let us go, he could not see how it was fair for him to rid himself of the Il Serpente pollution and allow his family to continue operating normally. That's why they killed him. They might have let my mother and my sisters go, but my father brought the authorities in. My uncle was forced to make an example of him." His mouth curved, but it was a bitter reenactment of that smile of his. "But I was here. He enjoyed making that example. He reveled in it."

This was where my childhood came in handy, I thought then. I could hear what he was saying. I could picture what he meant. I could want to cry again—for his life this time, instead of the death I'd imagined he'd walked into.

But I could also hold all of that inside.

"So what you're telling me is that you're not a monster at all," I said, as evenly as I could, because I wanted him to hear me say it out loud. Just in case he was ever tempted to try to sacrifice himself again. Just in case a dark day found him and convinced him that he was nothing but the thing his uncle made him. "You're the son of a hero and you lost your way."

"I found my way," Jovi told me, as if he was laying down law in the form of stone tablets. "I found my North Star, Rux. I found you."

"I thought you went to sacrifice yourself," I told him.

"You," he said, intensely, "would be worth sacrificing myself for, Rux. But I find I would rather have you than lose you."

I couldn't breathe. "But your vows. Your promises."

"I told you that you were mine and I was yours, *curò*," he said, even more urgently. "I meant that. You gave me your innocence and that meant something to me. You are my heart. It did not beat until I met you and now it only beats for you."

He was thundering all these things at me. They moved through me like a wild storm.

And I believed every word as surely as if they were written on my heart.

Because they were.

Jovi's gaze scanned mine, and it felt like that same thunder. "We have an hour."

"Until what?"

"I negotiated the terms of my exit from my family and from Sicily."

I wasn't sure I heard him properly. I wasn't sure I could believe him. That we had to run, that we had to escape, that made sense—but that they might let him go? Impossible.

Wasn't it?

I wanted it to be true more than I wanted my next breath. "I didn't think that was a possibility."

"Everything is a possibility if you have the proper tools," he told me. "In the case of my uncle, he underestimated the attention to detail I give to everything I do. Names. Places. Dates. Recordings. As if it was my job to maintain a record of his crimes."

"Did you always mean to leave Il Serpente, then?"

I hardly dared ask it. But he blinked, as if he'd expected the question. As if he'd asked it of himself.

"Tonight I dug up the graves inside of me," he told me gruffly. "I let the ghosts out, and all the memories that came with them. I tried to honor them. Yet all this time, I think that I was trying to honor my father in my own, twisted way. I told myself I was simply being thorough, and keeping myself safe. And I was. But I also think that I was gathering all the evidence my father would have. If he hadn't been found out. If he'd lived."

I was finding it hard to breathe. I was swaying, and my eyes were blurry again, but I couldn't seem to care enough to wipe at my cheeks.

Jovi reached over and did it for me. First one cheek, then the next. "But if you no longer wish to come with me, Rux—if you can't see a life with someone who's done the things that I have, I understand. I will get you out. But I will stay here and let them do what they will." He laughed, but it was a bitter sound that I didn't like at all. "I will take my place with the ghosts of this villa as I should have done years ago."

I slapped my hand in the center of his chest, shocking us both.

"We either both live or both die," I threw at him, intense and sure. As I had been about him from the start, hadn't I? As if I had recognized him the moment he'd appeared in my bedroom. As if my heart had known him at once. "And I'm not finished living, Jovi. I promised you right back. Yours." I pointed to myself. Then I pointed to him. "Mine."

And for a moment that I knew, somehow, would be etched into me forever, we stood there in the kitchen of his wreck of an old house and breathed each other in.

The vows we'd made wrapping tighter and tighter around us with every breath, just the way we liked it.

The way it had started. The way it would go on. The way it would end, he and I bound to each other like fate.

But not tonight. Not yet.

"They will be here within the hour," Jovi told me

after a small eternity passed between us. He leaned in and cradled my face in his hands. "You have brought me to life, my beautiful Rux. My *curò*, my light, my love. You showed me why the earth turns, why the birds sing, why the stars shine. I cannot be without you. I cannot bear it. I will not allow it."

"I love you, too," I whispered back, fiercely. "And I'm willing to fight for it. Even if the first one I have to fight is you."

He kissed me then. And it was dark and wild, filthy and deep. It was a ruthless, glorious claiming.

I kissed him back and I loved him so much it hurt.

"I never I doubted you." I whispered my confession in a rush. "I thought you had gone to die like some noble fool and I wanted you to feel as desolate as that made me."

For a moment, he only breathed. And I wished I could go back and do this differently.

"I'm sorry," I told him. "I—"

"Make no mistake," my love told me, his voice dark against my mouth. "I'll make you pay for that."

And we both smiled.

I pulled back, and it was my turn to get my hands on his face, to make sure he was looking at me with his whole beautiful soul in his eyes. "I love you, Giovanbattista. I love you, my Jovi. I will follow you anywhere."

"I love you, too," he told me in return, though it sounded as if the words hurt on the way out. He stared at me as if he couldn't believe he had said that. "I love you," he said again, more intensely that time. "I love you, Rux, and I will make sure you know it every day. Every single day that we have left, you and me."

"I don't care how we live or where," I said, kissing him again. "As long as it's with you. And as long as we live for as long as we can, as brightly as we can, together."

"I vow to you, we will." He intoned that as if he was standing at the front of a cathedral.

And I knew this man. I knew his heart, which meant I knew him better than anyone else on this earth, including him.

I knew if he vowed it, it was as good as done.

"Let's go," he said then. He took my hand and brought it to his mouth. "There is no forever here, and we've earned one. But there is one thing we have to do first."

Jovi pulled out the gasoline after taking the bag he'd kept packed for Rux to his car, and throwing his own in beside it. They both splashed it where they could, working fast and determinedly, because the clock was ticking.

"Are you sure?" Rux asked him when they were done, and all that was left was the lighting of a match. She was staring up at the villa, a curious look on her face. Not sad, not exactly. Aware, perhaps, of the finality of what they were doing here.

But he was looking only at her. "I have never been more certain of anything."

Still, it took a deeper breath than usual to do what needed to be done. To strike the match and let it arc through the dark to the ground. Then flare as it found the gasoline.

Then burn.

He watched the flames for a moment, remembering. Letting himself *remember*.

And letting himself let go. Of ghosts and memories, lives lost and lives half lived, vows and promises, family and loss. So much loss.

Then he led Rux to the car, made sure she was safely inside, and left the old villa behind him, flames climbing high. By the time his uncle and his cousin and their men made it halfway up the hillside—Jovi was certain he'd just missed running into them on the narrow road—the place was engulfed in fire.

A long-overdue funeral pyre in honor of his family, Jovi thought.

A fitting end to the long, sad story of Donatello D'Amato, who had longed for a better life than the one he'd been mired in on this island.

Leaving Sicily felt much the same. Too much darkness, too many ghosts.

And nothing ahead of them but possibility and the deep blue sea.

They boarded the boat he had waiting for them and set off, leaving the lights of Palermo behind them. And high on the hill in the distance, he could see the fire he'd set.

"They will think you're dead," Rux murmured, tucked up against his side.

"It is better, I think, that they do," he replied. But what he thought was, *They will wish that I am dead.*

And then, in the night, they will wake from their nightmares of me and know better.

A satisfying end, to his way of thinking.

It took him about a week into their new life—a lazy tour of whatever beaches took their fancy, easy enough to do when he'd laid out a trail involving flights to Perth, Australia, and a cabin in his name in the far-flung Solomon Islands, about as far away as a person could get from Sicily—for him to realize that his lovely Rux was under the impression that they were on the run. Living hand to fist and forever looking over their shoulder.

"You misunderstand," he told her as they lounged on the deck of the small yacht, having their dinner beneath the stars somewhere off the coast of Perpignan, France, near the border of Spain. "I'm a very wealthy man."

"Your uncle was," Rux said, nodding. "I understand that."

"I lived in an empty house," he reminded her. He stared at her until she blushed, one of his favorite new pastimes. "I spent my money on nothing. How do you think I got your passport in a couple of days? How do you think we've managed to effect our escape by means of a tranquil yachting holiday?"

"I..."

"I think," Jovi said, with a mock disapproval, "that we are going to have to decide on the appropriate punishment for such offensive behavior, *mia vita*."

My life.

Because that was exactly what she was. And would always be.

He watched her sigh happily as she came to him and arranged herself over his lap, so he could make sure they both enjoyed her punishment to the fullest.

In the life they were making together, all of the punishments were about love. They were made in love and they led to love. And really, they were just a way of playing their favorite games with each other as they wished.

Jovi intended to make certain that they could do this forever, because Rux deserved nothing less.

He had been very clear with his uncle. Should anything happen to him—or, God forbid, to Rux—or should he so much as feel the faintest tickle on the back of his neck to suggest that someone was following him, it would trigger an avalanche.

You think I'm afraid of an avalanche? Antonio had scoffed, malignant and furious in his little throne that day. *You ungrateful* cazzo.

It will come at you from all directions, Jovi had promised him, and it was not quite that he took pleasure in it, because too much was at stake. But all told, he would admit that it was probably the very best day he'd ever spent in that cursed house. *All your secrets, Ziu. Have you forgotten? I know exactly where all the bodies are buried. All this time you thought you owned me. That you made me. That I was your creature. All this time, the creature has owned you.*

I should have known that you would turn traitor, the old man had sneered. *It's in the blood.*

Your blood is a rotting carcass, Jovi had told him,

the way the old women muttered their curses. *And soon enough, the crows will come.*

Much as Antonio had tried to hide it, Jovi had seen a flicker in his gaze. An acknowledgment all of his relatives liked to make when they were deep in their *amari* at the end of a long meal—but did not much care to make at other times, when the inevitable felt closer.

That they would all die the way they lived, hard and mean. That the choices they made assured it. That they were signing their own death warrants in blood and misery.

Antonio had no sweet old age to look forward to and it had been clear he knew it. He'd never taken care of his body, and it had shown. The same way his evil deeds had shown in his eyes and all over his face. If he was lucky, his body would give out. Otherwise, it was as likely to be prison as it was to be an assassination—possibly at the hand of his own son.

They had stared at each other, Jovi and the man who had tried to make him in his twisted image. And he thought they had both seen the same grim future awaiting his uncle.

You know as well as I do that your blood and mine have nothing in common, except what you spilled of it, Jovi had told him quietly. Intently. *My father was an honorable man. He wanted better things than this. So do I. The difference is, I will walk away from Il Serpente the way he couldn't, and you will let me.*

Antonio had snarled at him. *Carlo will never stop looking for you.*

Carlo is a cowardly imbecile, Jovi had retorted. *He*

will never get close to me. If I were you, I would convince him that he's better off keeping his distance from even the thought of coming after me. Unless, that is, you don't want your disappointing successor around. Just let me know. I'd be happy to dispose of him, too.

His uncle had growled at him, but he had said nothing.

Damning Carlo with something that hadn't even risen to the level of faint praise.

Jovi had taken the time to outline all the many ways he could destroy his uncle with a phone call. Not that a phone call was necessary. If certain protocols weren't followed, by him and by Rux, it would trigger a cascade of consequences that he knew his uncle didn't want.

The old man listened, a sour look on his face, as Jovi spelled it all out for him. The investigators that would receive charts and dissertations. The journalists who would receive similar packages. The entire web he'd created to expose every single secret he knew about his family.

This is the cost of treating a nephew the way you treated me, Jovi had told him. *I learned to stay quiet. You forgot I was there. You have no one to blame but yourself, Uncle. You betrayed yourself. Over and over again.*

All of this, the old man had said, shaking his head. *All of this for some nameless girl.*

I know her name, Jovi had retorted. *But if I were you, I'd make certain never, ever to learn it.*

And he'd walked out the front door of that house they'd dragged him into, battered and bloody and wracked with grief, so many years before.

He took his Rux around the world. He showed her everything she'd ever dreamed of or read about, everything she thought she'd never see. When she woke from dreams that brought her back to old cages, he soothed her. And when his memories came to haunt him, she taught him how to make them stories that she laughed at and cried through, until he learned how to do the same.

They packed these travels into the first six months of their freedom, because afterward, she was too pregnant to travel that easily.

"I didn't give birth control a second thought," she said, laughing, the rounder she got.

"I told you I wanted you," he replied every time. "And I do. I want everything that comes with wanting you. Babies. Old age. All of it."

And when she smiled at him, he felt certain that he could hang the stars if she asked.

Five years after they left Sicily, they had a toddler named Bella and a baby named Alessandra, and, he suspected, another one on the way. They lived on a remote beach in New Zealand where they kept to themselves, loved each other deeply and totally, and marinated in the fact that they could do these things.

That they could be anything they liked.

Ten years on, Jovi had not relaxed his guard, but things had changed. His daughters and son were older and they'd moved closer into the village to take advantage of the schools and the community, so their children could have what they'd never had. Sometimes Jovi would watch his youngest, Luca Donatello, play rugby—happy and heedless, with nothing to worry about except winning—and feel that ache in his heart again.

But by then, he understood that ghosts were just another form of love. In some ways, the most enduring kind. And they sweetened over time—the more he allowed them access and told their stories. Sometimes they came and visited and he could really feel all the ways he'd changed. Not just inside himself, and the way he loved Rux more every day, but the fact that he'd disrupted the cycle.

His children were bright and silly. They were reckless and free. They complained about being bored and had the space to make up their own entertainments.

Every day, they had nothing to worry about but their own little lives. They had no concept of the great canopy surrounding them, the whole world that was out there, or the bad things that could happen in it.

They got to be kids, in other words. The way he and Rux never had.

Don Antonio D'Amato died of a heart attack while consorting with his mistress, but his bitterly loyal wife buried him in state, like he'd been taken while praying. Carlo died less than six months later, taken out in a fiery gunfight in a club in Palermo by his cousins, who resented his haphazard leadership.

Il Serpente shed its skin, but this time, with the help of some mysterious packages that arrived in police stations and at news channels, the snake did not rise again. Within a couple of years, there were more members of the D'Amato family behind bars than carousing in the usual Palermo hot spots.

Jovi took a long walk on the local beach and though he would never admit this to another living person save Rux, he had felt Donatello with him.

He thought, at last, that his father might have forgiven him for failing to save his sisters, his mother. And for who Antonio had made him.

He'd felt as certain as he could that Donatello might even be proud of him.

"Of course he is," Rux whispered fiercely that night, their naked bodies slick and tangled tight together. "He loves you. Then, now, and always, you foolish man."

And he'd taken great pleasure in punishing her for that impertinence.

Some twenty years after the night they'd climbed on that boat and left Sicily in their wake, their babies were grown enough to be in university or in the early stages of their careers, and so Jovi took his beautiful Rux to Buenos Aires for a season.

They danced on cobblestones and laughed into the night.

On one such night, filled with music and light, they walked back to the little flat he'd bought for them. There was no room for children. It was only theirs, and they were holding hands like they were young again as they whispered back and forth about all the things they planned to do to each other when they got back to the flat and closed the door behind them.

"I still can't believe you're real," Rux told him, smiling up at him. He had put a ring on her finger before their first daughter was born. They had spoken the vows that they had lived since the day they'd met, giving them that extra power. He liked to play with the sparkling stone as they walked, reminding him that she was his. Always his. "Sometimes I think I'll wake up in that bedroom in my father's house and find this was all a dream."

Boris Ardelean had met the unpleasant end he deserved. Rux's stepmother, on the other hand, was thriving. She had done very well indeed, helped along by a little judicious aid from Jovi over time. It was too dangerous to meet up with her, but somehow, Jovi thought that a woman like Katarzyna would understand how and why she had a very specific guardian angel.

When Katarzyna had proved this by managing to find a way to get Rux the only picture that she'd ever had of her mother, Rux had cried and cried. *I thought this was lost the way she was*, she'd told him. *This means more than you know.*

But he knew. He knew too well, as he'd watched his children grow up with the faces of those that he and Rux had lost. Only better, because they were entirely themselves.

And wholly free.

"It's not a dream," he told her as they walked, both of them shimmering with tango and local cocktails. "It's so much better than that, *mia vita*. It's our beautiful life. It's love. It's us."

Then he backed her up against the nearest wall and kissed her with all the passion they'd always had, and always would.

"You had better get me home," she told him, her arms looped around his neck. It was an order, and she delivered it with that smile of hers that was still the whole sun to him.

"As you wish," he murmured in reply, the way he always did.

And he hurried her back to the flat so he could get inside her, hold her close, and make sure she shined as bright as possible while she exploded all around him.

The way she always did, like fireworks.

Because the fire they'd made together never went out. It only got better.

And as long as they were together, all the rest of their days and the breaths that they took, it always would.

* * * * *

Did you fall in love with Sicilian Devil's Prisoner? *Then you're sure to enjoy these other sensational stories by Caitlin Crews!*

Carrying a Sicilian Secret
Kidnapped for His Revenge
Her Accidental Spanish Heir
Forbidden Greek Mistress
An Heir for Christmas

Available now!

Get up to 4 Free Books!

We'll send you 2 free books from each series you try PLUS a free Mystery Gift.

FREE Value Over **$25**

Both the **Harlequin Presents** and **Harlequin Medical Romance** series feature exciting stories of passion and drama.

YES! Please send me 2 FREE novels from Harlequin Presents or Harlequin Medical Romance and my FREE gift (gift is worth about $10 retail). After receiving them, if I don't wish to receive any more books, I can return the shipping statement marked "cancel." If I don't cancel, I will receive 6 brand-new larger-print novels every month and be billed just $7.19 each in the U.S., or $7.99 each in Canada, or 4 brand-new Harlequin Medical Romance Larger-Print books every month and be billed just $7.19 each in the U.S. or $7.99 each in Canada, a savings of 20% off the cover price. It's quite a bargain! Shipping and handling is just 50¢ per book in the U.S. and $1.25 per book in Canada.* I understand that accepting the 2 free books and gift places me under no obligation to buy anything. I can always return a shipment and cancel at any time. The free books and gift are mine to keep no matter what I decide.

Choose one:
- ☐ **Harlequin Presents Larger-Print** (176/376 BPA G36Y)
- ☐ **Harlequin Medical Romance** (171/371 BPA G36Y)
- ☐ **Or Try Both!** (176/376 & 171/371 BPA G36Z)

Name (please print)

Address   Apt. #

City   State/Province   Zip/Postal Code

Email: Please check this box ☐ if you would like to receive newsletters and promotional emails from Harlequin Enterprises ULC and its affiliates. You can unsubscribe anytime.

Mail to the Harlequin Reader Service:
IN U.S.A.: P.O. Box 1341, Buffalo, NY 14240-8531
IN CANADA: P.O. Box 603, Fort Erie, Ontario L2A 5X3

Want to explore our other series or interested in ebooks? **Visit www.ReaderService.com or call 1-800-873-8635.**

---

*Terms and prices subject to change without notice. Prices do not include sales taxes, which will be charged (if applicable) based on your state or country of residence. Canadian residents will be charged applicable taxes. Offer not valid in Quebec. This offer is limited to one order per household. Books received may not be as shown. Not valid for current subscribers to the Harlequin Presents or Harlequin Medical Romance series. All orders subject to approval. Credit or debit balances in a customer's account(s) may be offset by any other outstanding balance owed by or to the customer. Please allow 4 to 6 weeks for delivery. Offer available while quantities last.

Your Privacy—Your information is being collected by Harlequin Enterprises ULC, operating as Harlequin Reader Service. For a complete summary of the information we collect, how we use this information and to whom it is disclosed, please visit our privacy notice located at https://corporate.harlequin.com/privacy-notice. Notice to California Residents – Under California law, you have specific rights to control and access your data. For more information on these rights and how to exercise them, visit https://corporate.harlequin.com/california-privacy. For additional information for residents of other U.S. states that provide their residents with certain rights with respect to personal data, visit https://corporate.harlequin.com/other-state-residents-privacy-rights/.

HPHM25